HER LAST

HOPE

(A Rachel Gift Mystery—Book Three)

BLAKE PIERCE

Blake Pierce

Blake Pierce is the USA Today bestselling author of the RILEY PAGE mystery series, which includes seventeen books. Blake Pierce is also the author of the MACKENZIE WHITE mystery series, comprising fourteen books; of the AVERY BLACK mystery series, comprising six books; of the KERI LOCKE mystery series, comprising five books; of the MAKING OF RILEY PAIGE mystery series, comprising six books; of the KATE WISE mystery series, comprising seven books; of the CHLOE FINE psychological suspense mystery, comprising six books; of the JESSE HUNT psychological suspense thriller series, comprising nineteen books; of the AU PAIR psychological suspense thriller series, comprising three books; of the ZOE PRIME mystery series, comprising six books; of the ADELE SHARP mystery series, comprising thirteen books, of the EUROPEAN VOYAGE cozy mystery series, comprising four books; of the new LAURA FROST FBI suspense thriller, comprising six books (and counting); of the new ELLA DARK FBI suspense thriller, comprising nine books (and counting); of the A YEAR IN EUROPE cozy mystery series, comprising nine books, of the AVA GOLD mystery series, comprising six books (and counting); and of the RACHEL GIFT mystery series, comprising six books (and counting).

An avid reader and lifelong fan of the mystery and thriller genres, Blake loves to hear from you, so please feel free to visit www.blakepierceauthor.com to learn more and stay in touch.

BOOKS BY BLAKE PIERCE

RACHEL GIFT MYSTERY SERIES
HER LAST WISH (Book #1)
HER LAST CHANCE (Book #2)
HER LAST HOPE (Book #3)
HER LAST FEAR (Book #4)
HER LAST CHOICE (Book #5)
HER LAST BREATH (Book #6)

AVA GOLD MYSTERY SERIES
CITY OF PREY (Book #1)
CITY OF FEAR (Book #2)
CITY OF BONES (Book #3)
CITY OF GHOSTS (Book #4)
CITY OF DEATH (Book #5)
CITY OF VICE (Book #6)

A YEAR IN EUROPE
A MURDER IN PARIS (Book #1)
DEATH IN FLORENCE (Book #2)
VENGEANCE IN VIENNA (Book #3)
A FATALITY IN SPAIN (Book #4)

ELLA DARK FBI SUSPENSE THRILLER
GIRL, ALONE (Book #1)
GIRL, TAKEN (Book #2)
GIRL, HUNTED (Book #3)
GIRL, SILENCED (Book #4)
GIRL, VANISHED (Book 5)
GIRL ERASED (Book #6)
GIRL, FORSAKEN (Book #7)
GIRL, TRAPPED (Book #8)
GIRL, EXPENDABLE (Book #9)

LAURA FROST FBI SUSPENSE THRILLER
ALREADY GONE (Book #1)
ALREADY SEEN (Book #2)

ALREADY TRAPPED (Book #3)
ALREADY MISSING (Book #4)
ALREADY DEAD (Book #5)
ALREADY TAKEN (Book #6)

EUROPEAN VOYAGE COZY MYSTERY SERIES
MURDER (AND BAKLAVA) (Book #1)
DEATH (AND APPLE STRUDEL) (Book #2)
CRIME (AND LAGER) (Book #3)
MISFORTUNE (AND GOUDA) (Book #4)
CALAMITY (AND A DANISH) (Book #5)
MAYHEM (AND HERRING) (Book #6)

ADELE SHARP MYSTERY SERIES
LEFT TO DIE (Book #1)
LEFT TO RUN (Book #2)
LEFT TO HIDE (Book #3)
LEFT TO KILL (Book #4)
LEFT TO MURDER (Book #5)
LEFT TO ENVY (Book #6)
LEFT TO LAPSE (Book #7)
LEFT TO VANISH (Book #8)
LEFT TO HUNT (Book #9)
LEFT TO FEAR (Book #10)
LEFT TO PREY (Book #11)
LEFT TO LURE (Book #12)
LEFT TO CRAVE (Book #13)

THE AU PAIR SERIES
ALMOST GONE (Book#1)
ALMOST LOST (Book #2)
ALMOST DEAD (Book #3)

ZOE PRIME MYSTERY SERIES
FACE OF DEATH (Book#1)
FACE OF MURDER (Book #2)
FACE OF FEAR (Book #3)
FACE OF MADNESS (Book #4)
FACE OF FURY (Book #5)
FACE OF DARKNESS (Book #6)

A JESSIE HUNT PSYCHOLOGICAL SUSPENSE SERIES
THE PERFECT WIFE (Book #1)
THE PERFECT BLOCK (Book #2)
THE PERFECT HOUSE (Book #3)
THE PERFECT SMILE (Book #4)
THE PERFECT LIE (Book #5)
THE PERFECT LOOK (Book #6)
THE PERFECT AFFAIR (Book #7)
THE PERFECT ALIBI (Book #8)
THE PERFECT NEIGHBOR (Book #9)
THE PERFECT DISGUISE (Book #10)
THE PERFECT SECRET (Book #11)
THE PERFECT FAÇADE (Book #12)
THE PERFECT IMPRESSION (Book #13)
THE PERFECT DECEIT (Book #14)
THE PERFECT MISTRESS (Book #15)
THE PERFECT IMAGE (Book #16)
THE PERFECT VEIL (Book #17)
THE PERFECT INDISCRETION (Book #18)
THE PERFECT RUMOR (Book #19)

CHLOE FINE PSYCHOLOGICAL SUSPENSE SERIES
NEXT DOOR (Book #1)
A NEIGHBOR'S LIE (Book #2)
CUL DE SAC (Book #3)
SILENT NEIGHBOR (Book #4)
HOMECOMING (Book #5)
TINTED WINDOWS (Book #6)

KATE WISE MYSTERY SERIES
IF SHE KNEW (Book #1)
IF SHE SAW (Book #2)
IF SHE RAN (Book #3)
IF SHE HID (Book #4)
IF SHE FLED (Book #5)
IF SHE FEARED (Book #6)
IF SHE HEARD (Book #7)

THE MAKING OF RILEY PAIGE SERIES

WATCHING (Book #1)
WAITING (Book #2)
LURING (Book #3)
TAKING (Book #4)
STALKING (Book #5)
KILLING (Book #6)

RILEY PAIGE MYSTERY SERIES
ONCE GONE (Book #1)
ONCE TAKEN (Book #2)
ONCE CRAVED (Book #3)
ONCE LURED (Book #4)
ONCE HUNTED (Book #5)
ONCE PINED (Book #6)
ONCE FORSAKEN (Book #7)
ONCE COLD (Book #8)
ONCE STALKED (Book #9)
ONCE LOST (Book #10)
ONCE BURIED (Book #11)
ONCE BOUND (Book #12)
ONCE TRAPPED (Book #13)
ONCE DORMANT (Book #14)
ONCE SHUNNED (Book #15)
ONCE MISSED (Book #16)
ONCE CHOSEN (Book #17)

MACKENZIE WHITE MYSTERY SERIES
BEFORE HE KILLS (Book #1)
BEFORE HE SEES (Book #2)
BEFORE HE COVETS (Book #3)
BEFORE HE TAKES (Book #4)
BEFORE HE NEEDS (Book #5)
BEFORE HE FEELS (Book #6)
BEFORE HE SINS (Book #7)
BEFORE HE HUNTS (Book #8)
BEFORE HE PREYS (Book #9)
BEFORE HE LONGS (Book #10)
BEFORE HE LAPSES (Book #11)
BEFORE HE ENVIES (Book #12)
BEFORE HE STALKS (Book #13)

BEFORE HE HARMS (Book #14)

AVERY BLACK MYSTERY SERIES
CAUSE TO KILL (Book #1)
CAUSE TO RUN (Book #2)
CAUSE TO HIDE (Book #3)
CAUSE TO FEAR (Book #4)
CAUSE TO SAVE (Book #5)
CAUSE TO DREAD (Book #6)

KERI LOCKE MYSTERY SERIES
A TRACE OF DEATH (Book #1)
A TRACE OF MURDER (Book #2)
A TRACE OF VICE (Book #3)
A TRACE OF CRIME (Book #4)
A TRACE OF HOPE (Book #5)

CHAPTER ONE

To think, just the month before, Maria Ramirez's biggest worry was that she could not find a large enough pair of soccer cleats for her son. It had seemed like such a massive worry, making sure she had those dumb shoes before tryouts started. Her entire world had rotated around the search for those shoes for about three days. As she walked out of the hospital and toward the dark parking lot, the amount of stress that endless search for cleats had caused seemed almost comical.

Things had changed quite a bit since then and it had helped her to re-prioritize things that were important. Cleats. Soccer. Anything leisurely or fun…what was the point to any of it now?

Of course, she'd have to paint it in a totally different light for her two kids. She figured they'd understand it; they were just old enough to truly understand what her recent batch of bad news would mean for them. With the news she just received, things were going to look different. There would be some very hard conversations with the kids and their father. Maria and her ex-husband hadn't talked about anything for more than five minutes over the last three years, but they were going to have to now.

She felt the hospital looming behind her, almost like a haunted house in a badly made horror movie. The news she'd received inside had not been hopeful; it had been downright awful, actually. But she was choosing not to let it eat away at her. She was choosing to try to use it as a way to connect with her kids, to show them that life wasn't all about soccer cleats or getting a new Xbox because the old one overheated and broke.

She pulled out her phone, wanting to call Teddy, her son, to tell him to take some chicken out of the freezer. She had no idea what she'd make for dinner tonight, but she needed to get her mind on daily, routine things. Maybe over dinner, she'd tell them. It would be difficult and there would be some hard conversations over the next few days, but it needed to be done.

Thinking of the frozen chicken as she neared her car, she chuckled nervously. "To hell with that."

Maria figured given the news she'd just received she could take one night off from cooking. Besides, the kids had been asking for Chinese takeout for two weeks now. Maybe she'd treat them to soften the blow of what needed to be discussed.

Her cellphone glowed in the night as she stopped by her car, Googling the phone number of their favorite Chinese place. Before pressing the Call button, she tried to remember that weirdly named dish her son liked. "Moo shoo? Some kind of pork," she muttered.

With her eyes still on her phone, she just barely saw the figure come rushing around the front of her car. For a very strange moment, she thought it was a ghost—some odd amorphous shape moving through the night. But then she saw it was simply because the figure was dressed in all black. She saw the shape of a hood pulled over the head but that was it.

Before Maria could make sense of anything else, there was a blinding, sharp pain in her stomach. She opened her mouth to scream but could not draw any air. The dark figure in front of her seemed to grow darker as the pain continued.

Stabbed. I've been stabbed.

This fact came slamming home as the blade was drawn out. Maria fell against the side of her car, trying to draw in a breath while also trying to get a clear look at her attacker. Her eyes did fall on the attacker's face but it was quickly replaced by the shape of a knife that was stained with her own blood. She locked eyed with the killer for only a moment. She could tell it was a man because he was muttering something to himself. The voice was masculine and hurried. She could not tell what he was saying, but it certainly seemed like a one-sided conversation.

"…if I want to get it done…and quick…just do it and…"

This oddity distracted her long enough to miss the sight of the knife that came down and across her neck in a vicious slashing motion.

It felt almost like a papercut at first—a papercut and nothing more. But then it felt like her entire neck had been torn open and the last thing Maria Ramirez felt before she slid down the side of her car and to the pavement was her blood, warm and pumping freely, cascading down her chest. She could still hear the killer talking, which was odd, because even as the life poured out of her, she was quite certain her killer had been alone.

CHAPTER TWO

Rachel sat on her couch, in the middle of her quiet house, and looked to her daughter. Paige's eyes were shifting uncomfortably—something they'd been doing for the last day or so. Rachel could tell that Paige knew something was going on but was too afraid to ask. Paige Gift had always been the sort of kid that got easily embarrassed when others got into trouble. Even on television, she'd avert her eyes and sometimes cover her ears when people or even cartoon characters got into arguments.

So when she could sense there was tension or something out of balance within her own home, her mood shifted dramatically.

"Are you and Daddy upset with each other?" Paige asked.

Rachel did her best to never lie to her daughter, but she did know when to soften a blow. "In a way," she said. "It's just been a hard few days."

"Because of what you found in my room?"

Rachel nodded, reaching out and taking Paige's hand, "That's part of it yes."

On several occasions, Paige had tried explaining to Rachel how she felt about what had happened. She was still a little confused over what took place in her room two days ago. All Paige knew for sure was that she'd gone into her room and saw a dead squirrel on her floor. After that, given the reaction of both of her parents, she'd spent the next day or so swearing that she hadn't done it. She'd even requested that they have a funeral for the poor squirrel—which they had not been able to do because it had been taken as evidence.

Beyond that, Paige was more or less in the dark. Rachel, Peter, or any of the police or federal agents that had come through the house hadn't told her about the note that had been left with the squirrel. And really, it had been the note from Alex Lynch—presumably placed in Paige's room by an old friend or acquaintance of Lynch's—that had unnerved Rachel the most.

And later, when the police and FBI had left the house for the last time, Rachel and Peter had not told her about Rachel's diagnosis. In a hurried conversation between police visits and a wailing, agitated Paige, they'd made the decision to keep it between them for a few days—at least until the shock of the squirrel and the note had worn off. Even then, as they'd discussed the tumor immediately after the trauma of the dead squirrel, Rachel had felt something different between them. Something had shifted and it was never going to be the same.

"Mommy?"

"Yes, sweetie?"

"I know you're both upset and quiet…but can I watch a movie?"

"Sure."

She hated that Paige was so aware of the strain between them. Peter hadn't spoken to her very much in the past twelve hours. Rachel knew he was hurt and blindsided by the news about Alex Lynch, but he seemed devastated and angry about the fact that she'd not only been diagnosed with the tumor but that she'd kept it from him. He'd been cold and distant to her ever since they'd found the dead squirrel with the note in Paige's room. They'd had arguments before, even a shouting match or two, but this icy silence was something new. And it was made worse with the heaviness of her health diagnosis. It had been hard enough to finally tell him, but then with this Alex Lynch business right at the end of it, it was a whole different sort of turmoil.

She watched idly as Paige went to Disney Plus and started scrolling through some of her familiar favorites. She didn't realize until about twenty minutes into *Coco* that she was still holding Paige's hand and that her daughter's head was resting on her shoulder. A very sudden surge of emotion tore through Rachel and before she knew it, her eyes were watering with tears.

She blinked them back and subtly wiped them away, not wanting Paige to see. She already knew something was off between her parents. Seeing her mother—who rarely cried at all—crumple into a sobbing mess was only going to make matters so much worse.

"Hey, Rachel?"

She turned to the right, toward the kitchen, at the sound of Peter's voice. It was soft, nearly in a whisper. He looked a little more at ease than he had in the last two days, so that was good.

"Can we talk for a second, in the kitchen?" he asked.

Rachel nodded, then gave Paige a kiss on the forehead. Immersed in the movie, Paige barely noticed she had moved. Rachel walked into the kitchen, grabbed a water from the fridge, and sat at the bar. Peter did not sit. He stood on the other side of the bar, as rigid as a statue, and Rachel noticed for the first time that he looked scared. His dark hair was in disarray and his eyes looked uncertain—a rarity for Peter Gift. He almost looked like the nervous college sophomore she'd met so many years ago and it hurt her deeply—not the appearance, but the sting of the sweet memory.

"It's been a rough few days," he said simply.

"That's an understatement."

He furrowed his brow at this, as if upset that she'd dared to make such a flippant remark. "I've been thinking about it all day. *Literally* all day, trying to figure out what we need to do next in order to get over this. But I can't come up with anything because there are these two enormous obstacles. Not just one thing to get over, but *two*. And the more I think about them, the more I realize that you kept them from me."

"Peter, I know. But you—"

"You knew about the tumor for three entire weeks before you bothered telling me. You even went to visit Grandma Tate after getting the news and then came home upset about *her* diagnosis! You'd think that living through that would have spurred you on, but no. No, you kept it in…and I just can't figure out why."

"I had to process it myself, Peter. It was more than just telling you; it was telling Paige. And my God, I still have no idea how to—"

"I know. You've mentioned it numerous times in the last two days."

"Well, it's the only answer I have!"

She caught herself here, realizing how loud her voice was getting. They stared at one another for a handful of seconds, not speaking. She'd never seen him so angry before. It was chilling in a way she'd never quite experienced.

"But it's the Alex Lynch thing that really gets me," he said, also making sure to keep his voice low. "Somehow, he got to someone. He had someone break into our house and go into our daughter's room. And why? Because you paid him a visit and stirred shit up again!"

"Peter, you—"

"No," he shook his head and took a very deep breath. She noticed that he shuddered a bit when he let it out. He was really worked up. "I've spent the bulk of our marriage watching you throw yourself into your work, something I used to really admire and respect about you. But lately it's been too much—especially now that I know about the tumor. You chose to go out to work with that thing in your head before telling your husband and your daughter. That hurts in a way I can't even explain and…I don't…"

She reached out across the bar for his hand, but he would not give it to her. "Peter…"

He turned away from her, looking toward the kitchen sink. "I've spent the past half an hour or so packing a bag. I'm leaving, Rachel."

"What? You can't be seri—"

"This is all too much, and it's a double shot of proving how you've never put us first. It's always been work. And this tumor…you making the choice to not be treated for it? I love you, Rachel but that is the most selfish thing you can do. And I have no intention of just standing by and watching you die. And expecting Paige to do it is damn near monstrous."

Rage welled up in Rachel, but it was quickly overcome with the reality of what Peter was saying. As if sensing this, he said it again.

"I'm leaving. And I don't think I'll be coming back. We can discuss how things will work with Paige over the next few months, but not right now. Right now, I just need to be away from you."

"Peter, you can't…"

"I can and I am. I need to be away from you right now. I need to be alone."

And with that, he started up the stairs. Rachel wanted to call after him. She wanted to chase after him, to beg him to reconsider. But instead, she simply remained seated at the bar. She felt something start to come apart inside, an emotional wall that started to come down. She felt as if someone had reached into her stomach and tied her guts into knots.

Rachel sat there for a very long time, listening to the sounds of Paige's movie and the muffled sounds of Peter moving around upstairs. She didn't move until Peter was back down the stairs. He was carrying an overnight bag and his eyes were red. Apparently, he'd been crying upstairs.

"Peter…you don't have to do this."

He only shook his head at her and looked into the living room. "With the mood I'm in right now, I don't know if it's the smartest thing for me to take her with me. Can you be a present mother for another few days and be with her?"

"Yes." She wanted to lash out at him but deep down, she knew he was right. Still, her bitter tongue had to have its say. "Besides, your selfish decision shouldn't cause me to lose time with her."

"*My* selfish decision? Are you serious?"

But he was shaking his head again right away, not wanting to delve into an argument over it. "I'm going to check into a hotel. I'll text you when I'm settled." He headed for the door and turned back to her one last time. "You need to tell Paige about what's going on with you. The sooner, the better. Think of how you would have felt if Grandma Tate had kept it from you."

That said, he went out the back door quietly. He didn't say goodbye to Paige, and he didn't seem torn about it at all as he made his way out of the back door. Rachel knew this was unfair, though; he was likely hurrying out *because* it was so painful. She thought it was a rash and brutal decision, but she had to admit she could understand the pain of it all.

She remained in the kitchen for another five minutes, making sure she wasn't going to break. She knew she needed to respond emotionally but could not do it in front of Paige. She walked into the living room, where Paige was still watching her movie. "Hey, sweetie. I'm going to go upstairs for a minute, okay? And Daddy just left for a bit. Are you okay down here by yourself for a few minutes?"

"Yeah, Mom," she said, still starting at the television. She was so transfixed by the movie that she didn't even bother asking where her dad had gone.

Rachel started up the stairs and that sense of her house being one big tomb was stronger now. She wasn't sure where Peter was going or when he'd step foot back in the house again—if ever. It made the lonely feeling, the cumbersome sadness of every room and corner, so much worse.

"Hey Paige," she said, pausing at the bottom of the stairs. "What do you say we get out of here tomorrow. Just you and me? We'll take a trip to see Grandma Tate."

This snapped her out of her movie-trance at once. She leaped up on the couch and clapped her hands. "Grandma Tate? Yeah! Let's go!"

"Well, it's a long drive. Let me call her and we'll make sure it's okay first. And if she's good with it, we'll head down tomorrow."

Paige nodded, very excited, and plunked back down on her butt to watch the movie. Rachel had no idea if her spontaneous idea was a good one or a bad one, but having told Paige, it was too late to change her mind now. She briefly considered work, but she figured Anderson would surely not expect her to come in for a few more days, given everything that had gone down with Alex Lynch.

Slowly, Rachel went upstairs and retrieved her cell phone. She saw that she had a few texts from Jack. He'd been texting here and there ever since the dead squirrel had been found in Paige's room, just making sure she was okay. He was also letting her know that he was making damn sure everything humanly possible was being done to find out how Lynch had contacted someone from the outside to do such a thing.

Rachel chose not to read the texts just yet, instead going to her contacts. But as her finger hovered over Grandma Tate's number, that emotional wall came down faster and Rachel finally allowed herself a moment of weakness.

She fell onto her bed, buried her head into her pillow, and cried harder than she had in all her life. Behind all of the sorrow was the still-lurking anger towards Alex Lynch and a very tenuous set of plans as to how she might put a stop to whatever he was doing. Realizing there was no way she could actually have a conversation with Grandma Tate without her figuring out something was amiss, Rachel opted to text her. Through tear-streaked eyes, she typed in: *How do you feel about some visitors tomorrow? Just a day or two?*

She barely had enough time to wonder if it was almost rude to ask such a thing without any sort of lead-up before the response came through. She sometimes forgot just how quick Grandma Tate was to respond to texts.

Yes, please. Especially if Paige is part of the deal. When will you be here?

Rachel managed a thin smile, but as she typed in her response, she wondered if she was legitimately paying a visit to an ailing loved one, or if she was just running away.

CHAPTER THREE

They left the following day, and Rachel wasn't sure if she should be relieved by the fact that Paige had not asked why her father wasn't coming along. Maybe the girl was more observant than Rachel was giving her credit for, and even at a young age understood that something was off between her parents, and they needed some time away from one another.

Peter had texted the night before, letting Rachel know that he was checked into a Hilton. He'd be staying there for at least three days and going to work as usual. After that, he wasn't sure and would keep her posted. He'd step in and watch Paige for the foreseeable future, until they could work things out between them—whatever that looked like.

Rachel found herself reading through his texts again while standing outside of a fast-food restroom in Charlotte, North Carolina, waiting for Paige to come out. Paige was old enough now where she was embarrassed for Rachel to go into a public restroom with her, but Rachel was not comfortable with just letting her roam into a random McDonald's unattended.

As she waited for Paige, Rachel also checked the last texts from Jack. Reading through them, she was reminded how good of a friend Jack had always been—a solid friendship that was usually hidden under the formalities of their jobs. The last call she received from him told her that he'd personally spoken with the Richmond chief of police that was responsible for stationing two men in front of her house at all times.

You're safe, he'd texted. *And you'll remain safe until this is all over. We're looking hard into who may have broken into your home. Director Anderson sent some agents to visit Lynch to get him to talk. No luck so far.*

When Paige came stepping out of the restroom, Rachel put her phone away and smiled down to her daughter. "All good to go?"

"Yeah. Mom, you didn't have to come in."

"Oh, yes I did," she said, and in the back of her head, she saw that dead squirrel vividly.

***

Miraculously, Rachel was able to complete the drive to Aiken, South Carolina, without stopping for more bathroom breaks. Grandma Tate greeted them warmly, waiting for them on her front porch. Rachel noticed that when Paige hugged her grandmother, she did so very cautiously. She still didn't understand quite what was wrong with Grandma Tate—just that she was sick and it was a serious sort of sick that might not always look too bad.

"I don't know what your parents have told you," Grandma Tate told Paige, "but things aren't *that* bad yet. Now how about giving me a proper hug?"

As Rachel watched them embrace, she was reminded of how Paige had found out about Grandma Tate's diagnosis in the first place. It had been Peter, telling her in an almost causal way while she, Rachel, had been out of town on a case. It was a wretched feeling, but in that moment, she hated him a bit and was glad he'd stepped out.

Grandma Tate led them inside and right away, Rachel knew how the visit was going to go. Grandma Tate was going to do everything she could to make sure it was a fun trip—to make sure no sad or awkward conversations popped up. She'd already taken out some of Paige's favorite board games, stacked on the coffee table and waiting to be opened. She'd also taken out an old cookbook and insisted that Paige help her learn to finally make a cheesecake that doesn't fall apart.

Rachel smiled through it all, all the way up to that afternoon when they ended up in the back yard, playing a very sloppy and unorthodox game of croquet. She understood the need for distraction and deflection. After all, Grandma Tate and Paige still didn't know about her diagnosis. On top of that, she had no intention of telling her grandmother that it appeared her marriage might also be over. As for the unfortunate event of the dead squirrel in Paige's room, there was no way in hell she was talking about that. She'd even had a discussion with Paige on the way down about how they shouldn't tell Grandma Tate about it because it would only make her worry; and worrying was not something she should be doing in her current state.

The drive down had taken its toll on Rachel, so when the Candyland board was pulled out after dinner, she opted to just relax on the couch while Paige and Grandma Tate played. She thought of how ironic and odd it was that, somehow, she and Grandma Tate had right around the same amount of time left to live. And if Peter was indeed out of the picture, what did that mean for the amount of time she and

Grandma Tate might have together? As far as Rachel was concerned, Grandma Tate could spend a few weeks with her and Paige.

But there were other things to be considered as well, of course. If she had about a year or so left, how many of those weeks would she be able to spend working? How much of that time would she still have full and functioning control of her body? A year went by pretty damned fast, and she needed to make some hard decisions sooner rather than later. Right now, watching Paige giggle as Grandma Tate had to go back several spaces on the board, Rachel knew she wanted to spend as much time with her daughter as possible.

So I'll quit, she thought. *I'll quit work. I've got a pretty decent nest-egg saved up. I think it might work.*

It was an irresponsible thought and it scared her. She figured she could work for one more month, maybe get another case or two under her belt. She'd likely have to tell Anderson and those over him about her condition if she hoped to have any sort of financial assistance—and that was yet another thing she wasn't completely informed on, either.

Rachel did her best to shut those thoughts out, trying to focus on Paige and Grandma Tate. It worked for the most part, and she was able to make it through the rest of the evening as happy and as normal as she could. Yet, when Paige retired to bed and she was about to tell Grandma Tate just how tired she was, her grandmother stopped her.

"Everything okay, Rachel?"

"Yeah, just tired. That drive and then all of your games…it does a number on a girl."

"You sure? I may be old and quickly coasting to the Great Beyond, but my brain is pretty sharp, still. I mentioned Peter twice today and both times, Page got quiet for about ten minutes, Sort of sad. So, I ask again…is everything okay?"

"Oh, yeah. He's been working a lot and the last case I was on sort of took it out of me. We've been bickering a bit here and there, more than usual. I thin Paige has just picked up on it."

It's amazing and sad how good of a liar you are, she told herself.

"I think Paige might be a little scared of me," Grandma Tate said.

"How so?"

"Not *of* me, really. Just…she's aware that I'm going to die soon, so she's treating me like I'm made of porcelain. Have you gone in deep on what exactly is wrong with me?"

"Not too deep," Rachel said. And for a moment, she felt as if someone were tearing her heart out. it was almost like she and her grandmother were talking in code about her own condition. "We've

11

talked about what cancer is and how aggressive it can be, but that's about it."

"Do you think it might help her a bit if she hears some of it from me?"

"I don't know. But you're more than welcome to try having that conversation with her tomorrow." Secretly, though, it was the last thing Rachel wanted. She knew it was foolish, but she couldn't help but think that the more Paige knew about Grandma Tate's condition, the more likely she was going to be able to see right through her deceptions. "How about you?" she added. "Are you doing okay?"

"I am. Honestly, the worst part of it seems to be psychological. I feel like I'm supposed to be more upset that I was dealt this hand. But right now, I just don't care. I'm sure that will change as my health worsens, though." She shrugged and looked to the hallway behind Rachel. "Go on and get some sleep. I'll be up for another hour or so yet."

"Oh, well then I can keep you company."

She shook her head and smiled. "No. I love you, dear, but you look like death walking."

Rachel knew it was just euphemism for "you look tired" but it stung, nonetheless. It felt like Grandma Tate knew something, as if their cancers had telepathically linked them and Grandma Tate just *knew.* The feeling slid away, though, and Rachel retired to bed. As she brushed her teeth in the guest bathroom, she looked into the mirror and that comment rang over and over in her head.

"You look like death walking."

The alarming thing was that with the recent events with Peter and Alex Lynch's morbid gift, she was starting to *feel* like it, too.

***

Rachel woke up to the sounds of Paige giggling and the soft murmur of Grandma Tate's voice. She could also hear the faint hiss of water running in the kitchen sink, and a beeping noise she thought might be the microwave. With no bedside table in the guest bedroom, Rachel grabbed her phone and saw that she had somehow managed to sleep until 8:00 a.m. Apparently, her daughter and grandmother were making breakfast.

She got dressed and ran through her morning routine—always an odd feeling in someone else's bathroom, even if it was a family member's house. She hurried out to the kitchen, lured in by the smell of frying bacon, cheesy eggs, and coffee.

"Hey, it's Mommy!" Paige said. She was standing on a little footstool, helping Grandma Tate scramble a pan of eggs. "Hey, Sleepyhead!"

"Hey yourself, little chef." She then looked to Grandma Tate apologetically. "Sorry for sleeping in."

"Oh, shut your mouth. When was the last time you slept in past seven?"

"It's been a while," Rachel admitted as she fell in to help them with breakfast.

They ate breakfast together, with Grandma Tate asking Paige limitless questions about school, her pee-wee soccer league, and the sort of music and movies she was interested in. Rachel rarely spoke up, not because she was uninterested but because she wanted to make sure the two of them got in all of the conversation possible. She watched the ease with which Grandma Tate spoke to Paige, as if the death that was rapidly coming to claim her wasn't even on the radar. It made her envious, but it also solidified her decision not to tell Grandma Tate. She had her own hell to worry about in the coming months. Why make it harder with the news of her granddaughter also being taken out of the world far too early?

After breakfast, the three of them ventured out into the little cluster of flowerbeds along the backside of the house, just below the patio—the very same patio on which Grandma Tate had revealed her cancer to Rachel less than two weeks ago. Grandma Tate showed Paige how she pruned back certain bushes, how to tell when it was time to add new potting soil to the flowers, and then had her pick a small bouquet to put on the kitchen table. Paige enjoyed every single moment of it, particularly because it was the rare occasion where she was actually allowed to get her hands filthy.

After a game of Go Fish on the patio, Rachel snuck inside to make lunch. Grandma Tate had tried to take the duty, but Rachel insisted; she wanted her to have as much alone-time with Paige as possible. Besides, lunch was going to be nothing more than ham and cheese sandwiches, potato chips, and cut-up strawberries. It wasn't going to be a taxing process.

Yet, as Rachel was cutting the tops off of the strawberries, her phone began to buzz in her front pocket. She put the knife down and reached for the phone right away, her heart telling her that it must be Peter. He caller display, however, showed a different number. It was one she was overly familiar with and, though it instantly caused her some unease, she answered it anyway.

"This is Gift."

"Agent Gift, it's Director Anderson. How are things going on your end? I hope you've managed to find some solace after the last few days you've had."

Solace, she thought. *That's hilarious. And he doesn't even know about how things are going with Peter.*

"I don't think I'd use the word 'solace,' sir. Have there been any leads or connections made into who may have broken into my house and placed a dead squirrel in my daughter's room?"

"We do, in fact, have a few leads. And once things have settled and we have some more answers, I'll invite you into that case. As of right now—"

"I know, sir. I'd be too close to the case. Look, I really do appreciate you calling to check in on me, but I'm visiting with my—"

"That's not the only reason I called, Gift," he sounded irritated, perhaps because she'd just interrupted him. "I have a case I need you and Rivers on."

"A case? Sir, I'm dealing with a lot here, and I'm not even home right now. I'm visiting my grandmother in South Carolina."

"Well come back. Listen, I considered just sending Rivers by himself, but I think this is a case the two if you could wrap quickly. It seems to fit nicely with the last few you've worked on."

"Sir, I…"

But she stopped here, as her heart seemed to communicate something to her brain. It was what she supposed some people might refer to as an *a-ha* moment. She knew right away that she would not outright refuse the case. Over the last three days, she'd felt lost. Coming to visit with Grandma Tate had helped that but there were still secrets she was keeping, still worries and fears about her future that had gone uncommunicated with everyone. It had her feeling lost and useless. And she knew the only thing that had ever truly made her feel fully in control, and as if she had a sense of purpose, was her work.

Besides, if she was being selfishly honest, a simple case would be a welcome distraction. "Where's the case?"

"Roanoke. We've got two bodies already. There will be more information during the debrief."

"Yes, sir. But, as I said, I'm in South Carolina. So, it might be a while." Another obstacle which she didn't mention to Anderson was that she wasn't so sure Peter would be very accepting of needing to watch Paige while he was apparently living out of a hotel.

He sighed, and even without the vocal expression of a word, it was clear that he was still irritated. "Well, how soon can you get here?"

Rachel looked to the bowl she'd been filling with strawberries and heard Paige and Grandma Tate talking outside, Paige letting out one of her telltale giggling fits. She knew deep down in her heart that it should be a harder decision to make, but everything in her told her to take the case. In a perfect world, she could just leave Page here with Grandma Tate for a few days but knowing that her grandmother could fall ill any day *and* that she and Peter were having issues made that an impossibility.

"Gift?"

"I don't know, sir. It's a seven-hour drive back home and I'll need to figure out something to do about my daughter."

"Fine. Just...I'm going to set up a conference for six o' clock tomorrow morning. I need you and Rivers here. If we don't get agents on the scene by lunchtime tomorrow, it's going to be messier than it needs to be."

"Yes, sir."

She ended the call, grateful that Anderson had essentially given her the rest of the afternoon and even a few hours of sleep tonight. Now came the hard part: telling Paige they were going to have to end the visit to Grandma Tate's a day short.

CHAPTER FOUR

"You've got to be kidding, Rachel!"

Peter's voice through the phone sounded almost like a snake, a hissing sort of anger that was somehow pinched as it came through the phone. Also, she was so accustomed to him calling her *Rach*—a living little nickname between them—that her entire name coming out of his mouth sounded strange.

She and Paige were currently in North Carolina, about half an hour from the Virginia state line. Paige was sitting in the back, preoccupied with a diner dash-style game on Rachel's iPad, while Rachel was speaking to Peter. Paige had her little earbuds in, listening to the orders being placed by a cartoon panda and his duck sidekick. This was a relief, as it meant she would not hear the conversation that was to come. Rachel had just told him about the call from Anderson and he was not taking it well.

"I'm not kidding. Besides, when things got hard, you ran off to focus on your job, right? I'm doing the same."

"That's not fair."

"I agree, and I'm sorry for that. But your job is there, near home. I can call the sitter and set all of that up for you. But as of five o' clock tomorrow morning, I'm going to be unavailable for a few days."

"So, in other words, nothing new."

"Nothing new," she parroted, snapping at him. It hurt because she knew there was a bitter core of truth to it.

"Then go ahead and call the sitter," he said. Rachel could not be sure, but she thought she heard a slight tremor of emotion in his voice. "Maybe this is for the best. If we don't want to dump this on Paige right away, things need to seem as if they're the same. Mommy and Daddy both drowning themselves in work. That's about the norm, right?"

She didn't necessarily see this as a slight against her, but of their style of parenting. Because he was right. Yes, Rachel had often wondered if Paige would grow up feeling as if she, Rachel, had never been there for her because she was always working. But to hear Peter come out and admit to the same thing in such a roundabout way was a bit more shocking than she expected.

"So how do you want to do it?" Rachel asked. She looked up into her rearview and saw that Paige was still caught up in her game, the earbuds still in. Still, if a quiet moment happened on the game, she may hear bits and pieces of the conversation. As of right now, though, she seemed fully distracted.

"I'll be home by seven," he said. "I'll bring pizza—the kind from Al's Pizza that she likes so much."

"You might get there before we do, but we won't be far behind you." A thought came to her, one that cut out her heart and nearly made her gasp in shock and surprise, but it made perfect sense. She chose her words carefully, not wanting to inadvertently fill Paige in on all that was going on between her mother and father if a quiet part came up on the game. "Peter, I think you need to stay there. I should be the one to…well, to go somewhere else."

"Don't be ridiculous, You can—"

"No. It just makes sense. You're right. I have this case and I'm always on the go anyway. So for things to seem stable…yeah. You be the one to stay there."

"You're sure about that?"

"Yes."

"And what happens if you get sick, Rachel? What happens when that tumor decides it's time for you to go?"

"We've still got a while."

"And you know this means you'll see less of Paige, right? You know you—"

"Yes, I know. And that's okay for now." She felt herself on the verge of totally breaking down, and she knew she had to get him off of the phone in order to prevent it. "We'll talk more about it later. Bye for now."

And with that, she ended the call. Rachel knew that Paige wasn't listening in, but Rachel felt that she had to save appearances anyway. She spoke to the dead line, stating: "Sounds good. Love you, too."

She then set the phone down in the center console and spent the next ten minutes staring ahead at the road in front of her, trying to keep more tears from falling.

***

Peter was still asleep on the couch when Rachel slipped out the next morning. She'd made a big production out of bedtime with Paige the night before, knowing she would not see her daughter before she left to

17

meet with Anderson and Jack. Rachel slipped into her thin coat before leaving the house, looking back to Peter once more. She thought about going over to him and telling him goodbye, to maybe even suggest they try to talk things through when she returned.

But his decision to sleep on the couch had affected her more than she realized. It had hurt in about ten different ways, none of which she could clearly focus on as she left the house. She was also concerned that in his anger and frustration with her, he may tell Paige about her diagnosis. Yes, it seemed like a monstrous thing to do, but he'd done so with Grandma Tate's diagnosis. Rachel figured she'd just have to assume that beyond his anger, he was the good and honest man she'd fallen in love with and married. There was no sense in worrying about it now.

She made the twenty-minute drive to work in silence—no radio, no audiobooks or podcasts. It just seemed fitting for everything that she was going through. Her mind was a myriad of thoughts and scenarios with no real direction. When she parked in the back of the building (a perk to being there so early), her mind was somehow on the image of Paige and Grandma Tate picking flowers out in the back yard, little bugs flying here and there around them while Paige sank her hands deep into the dirt.

She made her way to Anderson's reserved conference room, not at all surprised to find that Jack was already there, sipping on a coffee. She knew he was something of a night owl, but a human being able to operate at such a high level at six in the morning seemed unreal to her. As for Anderson, already at the head of the table with an opened folder in front of him, that was easier to believe. For a while now, Rachel had been convinced the man simply never slept.

For the most part, though, Anderson was an easy man to work for. Rachel knew she sometimes made risky decisions and caused him undue stress, but he'd never come down hard on her. He could come off as rude sometimes, and this morning seemed to be one of those times. As soon as she came into the room, he slid the folder to her. She saw that Jack already had one. As she picked it up, Jack gave her a playful look that seemed to say *Ooh, you're in trouble!*

"Before you look in that folder," Anderson said, "I need to know if you're capable of handling it, Gift. I know you have a ton going on at home right now, but I assure you, we have you covered. There are cops parked in front of your house twenty-four-seven for the next two days. And, as I told you on the phone, we have a team of men looking into Lynch and how he got someone into your house. I will update you as soon as I can on that. But if your mind is going to be back here, at home, tell me now."

"I'm fine, sir, though it would have been good to hear that part yesterday when you implied that I didn't have a choice."

Anderson looked over to Jack, giving him a quick frown. "Agent Rivers and I discussed your situation this morning before you came in. We may not agree totally on things, but he did point out the weight of your situation—your daughter, your husband."

"You will keep men around my home while I'm gone?"

"Yes."

She nodded and opened the folder. "Then I'm fine."

"Good," he said, and then carried on with business as usual. "We've got a situation developing out in Roanoke. Two bodies in the past five days, both killed in the proximity of medical centers. Evidence points to a potential serial based solely on how the victims were killed. Local PD have zero leads and, as is the case here at the bureau, are slightly understaffed; Gift, as you know, the bureau is experiencing this same staffing shortage and it's the primary reason I wanted you on this. Not only that, but this case seems to align with cases involving medical centers and the two of you working together have some experience there.

"Sad to say, that's all I have. Local police requested help yesterday and they obviously didn't get it from us, so get there are soon as you can."

"That's it?" Rachel asked.

"That's it. Please keep me updated on your progress."

Rachel and Jack nodded to one another and started for the door. On the way out, Anderson spoke up, almost hesitantly, as if he wasn't sure if he wanted to say anything at all. "Agent Gift, can I speak to you for a moment?"

"Yes, sir."

Jack made his way out, case folder in hand, closing the door behind him. When he was gone, Anderson got to his feet and studied Rachel in a way she'd often seen Jack resort to.

"Agent Rivers has your back," Anderson said. "If you ever have any doubt of that, shut it down right away. He spoke to me in a way a field agent should not speak to a Deputy Director when I suggested you had no real excuse to not take the case. As you may know, I have no children so I can't imagine what it was like for you to find that grisly surprise from someone linked to Lynch. If I seemed nonchalant about it, I apologize."

"Thank you, sir. But it's okay. Really."

"Another thing, though…Agent Rivers says that he fears there may be something else going on. He says you seemed distracted last time you worked together. He hinted that there might be an illness in your family but, respecting your privacy, told me none of it. If you're in need of a therapist, the bureau works with many different—"

"No, sir," she said. "I'm good. If anything, working this case will allow me to get away from some of the personal matters that…"

She stopped here, realizing that he and Jack didn't even know about her diagnosis. She also wasn't quite sure how to feel about the fact that he'd revealed the illness in the family to Anderson. She wasn't mad, just unsettled. It was a strange feeling.

Anderson nodded when she did not finish her sentence. "Understood. And I meant what I said: I'm making sure your family is being watched and kept safe."

"Thank you."

She turned and left before the conversation could get any odder. She found Jack sitting out in the small waiting area outside of Anderson's office. It was still so early that the receptionist hadn't arrived yet. But through the blinds, early morning sunlight peered through.

"Everything good?" Jack asked.

"Yeah. I was just being reminded of how great my partner is."

"Ah," he said, looking away in slight embarrassment. "Well, I could have told you that. We didn't need Anderson to relay it."

"I imagine there would be more truth coming from him."

"Ouch. I keep forgetting how crabby you can be in the morning."

"And we still have a two-and-a-half-hour drive ahead of us. Lucky you."

They headed down to fill out paperwork to take out a bureau car. Between then and actually getting behind the wheel, she found herself constantly thinking back to Paige—Paige asleep, Paige sticking her tongue out in concertation as she lined up a shot for croquet in Grandma Tate's back yard, Paige knowing nothing of her diagnosis.

You have to tell her, she told herself. *You have to tell her as soon you can. You should have already told her but, well, here we are…*

Yes, here we are. And right now, there was a case to solve. She'd interrupted her trip to see Grandma Tate for this, so she was going to set her mind on the case before cluttering it up with the mess she had left back at home.

20

"How's your grandmother?" Jack asked. "That's where you were when Anderson called yesterday, right?"

"She's fine. I took Paige down to see her. It went pretty well…until Anderson called, of course."

"And what about the elephant in the car that is this whole Lynch and his dead squirrel situation? Are you wanting to talk that out or do we leave it alone?"

She appreciated him asking. Over the past two cases, he'd noticed something was wrong with her and she'd snapped at him far too many times. He was trying his best to respect her privacy while still remaining a supportive partner.

"I think I'm leaving it alone for now. I can't let that creep occupy too much of my time if I'm on a case…despite the mistake I made of consulting with him in the first place. If Anderson gives me his word that he has people staking out my house and family, that's all the security I need for right now."

Only, as she drove farther away from the office and her home, she wondered if this was true. Paige was, after all, already weighing heavy on her mind. It had never been easy to leave Paige and Peter behind, but it was harder this time Maybe it was because of the secret she was keeping, but Rachel almost felt as if she were betraying her daughter.

Just another reason to just tell her when she got back home. But first, as always (as Peter might bitingly say), there was a case to close.

CHAPTER FIVE

Rachel drove directly to the site of the second crime scene as Jack once again read over the few case notes on his phone. When they arrived on the scene, a local deputy was already waiting for them. It was just shy of 8:30 and the city was filled with the noises of morning traffic. Roanoke, Virginia, was not a booming metropolis by any means, but it felt just as big as Richmond as people were zooming to work and doing other morning errands.

The crime scene was the parking lot of a small hospital. The lot was two levels, the primary level running adjacent to the hospital grounds and the second lot sitting at the bottom of a hill, connected by a set of concrete stairs built into the hillside. This lower-level parking lot was where they met the Roanoke Deputy, a middle-aged African American man with graying hair and the beginnings of what Rachel had always referred to as a pot belly. He seemed like a pleasant enough fellow, but he looked tired and a bit distressed.

"Good morning, agents," he said as Rachel and Jack met him by the hood of his patrol car. "Deputy Jerome Stanhope. Good to meet you."

"Agents Rivers and Gift," Jack said, stepping forward to shake the man's hand. Somewhere further ahead of them, an ambulance was dispatched, rolling out with its sirens blaring. Deep down, though she knew it was ridiculous, Rachel wondered if it was for her. She figured maybe it was just a reaction she'd have until her final days, hearing ambulance sirens and assuming it was some sort of glimpse of her future.

"So what do you know about the case?" Stanhope asked them.

"Just what the local PD told our Director," Jack said. "I mean, we've got the case notes, too, but there's not too much to go on. Two murders that seem to be the same in approach. One significantly worse than the other."

"Our reports say both bodies had their throats slashed," Rachel said. "But this most recent victim also had a deep stab wound in her stomach."

"That's right," Stanhope said. "Her name was Maria Ramirez, and she was leaving an appointment when she was killed. She had the last appointment of the day, meeting with Dr. Fenton. But I will say right now that the first victim was a bit more than just a simple throat-slashing. It was pretty brutal. At least six stab wounds from what I hear, and none of them were neat or clean."

"Well, if that's the case, why are we thinking they were linked at all?" Jack asked. "Why assume it's the same killer?"

"Forensics thinks it was likely the same weapon at both scenes. Also, the close proximity of the bodies to medical facilities."

"And what about Mrs. Ramirez?" Rachel asked. "Do we know what the appointment was for?"

"Not yet. The docs here are pretty rigid about patient confidentiality. We've put in a warrant for the records, though. I expect for everything to pass through by the end of the day."

"Was the family any help?" Jack asked.

"Not especially. It was news to them that she even had the appointment. It's an estranged ex-husband and a son of eleven. The only other local family is a grandfather but he's in a nursing home in Norfolk with some pretty severe Alzheimer's."

Rachel started to slowly scan the site of Maria Ramirez's murder as Jack continued asking questions. She listened in as she had a look around, though it was the sort of scene that told her right away it wasn't going to have much to offer. The lot itself merged with a simple two-lane road that bordered the side of the hospital before leading into a parking garage.

"And the first victim," Jack said, "was a sixty-year-old man by the name of Bruce Webber, correct?"

"Yeah, but I had nothing to do with that crime scene," Stanhope said. "That one wasn't at a hospital, but outside of a specialist's office. Real butchered-up and bloody."

None of this was news to Rachel. She'd read about the murder and the scant details of the scene in the report—or, rather, had Jack read them to her while she drove between Richmond and Roanoke. Webber seemed to have been the victim of a vicious and violent attack while Ramirez's case had been much more methodical. Still, Rachel listened to the back and forth between Jack and Stanhope, seeing if some new detail might be uncovered.

"It was a hepatologist, right?" Jack asked.

"Yeah, I think so. That's like a liver specialist, right?"

"Correct."

"From what we can tell on that one," Stanhope said, "the victim, Mr. Webber, was headed *to* an appointment. The specialist and his employees…none of them ever saw him that day. He never made it to his appointment. It was a patient coming out of the office that found Mr. Webber, dead in front of his car. We assume he was headed in when he was killed. No witnesses, no security footage, nothing."

Rachel took one last scan of the area but the only thing she found that was of any interest at all was a stained spot along the pavement that she thought might be blood from Maria Ramirez's body.

"Deputy Stanhope, would you please share the contact information of the immediate family?" she asked.

"Absolutely," he said. "I figured you'd need it. I've got it all printed out, waiting in the car. You think you'll need an assist?"

"It's unlikely," she said as Stanhope retrieved the folder and handed it to her. "But we'll certainly let you know if it comes to that."

"Well, if that's the case," the Deputy said, "I think I'm going to leave you to it. I've got about a dozen places I need to be at once—but seriously, just give me a ring if you need anything. My number is in there with the family contact information."

As Stanhope got back into his car, Rachel opened the folder he'd given her. There were only two contacts—one for each victim—and, as he'd said, his own cell phone number.

"He said there was some tension and weirdness between the estranged husband and Maria Ramirez," Rachel said. "I say, her being the most recent victim, we wait a bit. I think we speak to the Webber family first before we give the trail time to get cold."

"Sounds like a plan," Jack said as he also started to look around the area. He pointed to the light pole closest to them, frowning. "You notice how there are only two security lights down on this end of the lot?"

"I did. It would certainly be pretty easy for someone to hide, especially if it had just gotten dark. The question then becomes whether or not the killer was being opportunistic or if they were specifically out to get Mrs. Ramirez."

"And if so," Jack said, "are there any solid connections between Ramirez and Webber?"

Rachel nodded, already heading back to their car. "Let's go find out."

***

Bruce Webber had left behind a wife, three children, and one grandchild. When Rachel and Jack arrived at the Webber residence, two of the children were there to comfort their mother. The eldest, a man of thirty-five, answered the door with slow and methodical care. Rachel could tell that he was tired and still in the process of properly dealing with his grief.

"Agents Gift and Rivers," Rachel said, showing her badge at the doorstep. "We were hoping to get in some questions about what happened to Mr. Webber."

"Yeah, sure. The police said there might be some FBI folks coming by," he offered his hand out of nothing more than some basic, programmed response. Rachel and Jack both shook it as they entered while the man introduced himself.

"I'm Tommy Webber, and my mom is Eloise. She's in the kitchen right now, finally eating. She's better today, but still out of it."

"That's certainly understandable," Rachel said. "Well do our best not to take too long."

Tommy led them through the house, a modest two-story in a neighborhood where a lot of the homes looked pretty much identical from the outside. They passed by a small den, where a piano sat off in the corner all alone, before coming to the kitchen. There, they found an older woman and a younger woman that was unmistakably her daughter at work behind the stove and a cutting board.

"Mom," Tommy said as they entered, "the FBI agents are here."

The older woman, currently stirring something in a large pot on the stove, turned to greet them. She smiled in the same tired way Tommy had. Her hair was out of sorts and her eyes, though wide by design, looked wiped out. The older woman set the spoon she was stirring with down on the side of the stove and walked around the small island to greet them.

"Hi, I'm Eloise Webber. Thanks so much for coming by." She turned and looked almost apologetically at the stove. "We're making Brunswick stew—a little odd for so early in the morning, but it was Bruce's favorite. We felt it was sort of appropriate."

"Mrs. Webber," Jack said, "I am of the firm opinion that no one should ever apologize for making stew."

The smile that touched the corner of Mrs. Webber's lips was genuine, though brief. It was yet another reminder of just how good Jack was with people. Rachel often prided herself on her bedside manner, but Jack had a way of setting people at ease in just about any sort of situation.

The daughter spoke up then, finally setting down her knife and gently pushing a pile of chopped carrots to the side. "I'm Jade," she said. "Like Mom said, thanks for coming by. It's been hard these last few days."

"Of course," Rachel said. "Now, all we know from the initial police report was that Mr. Webber was headed to an appointment with a hepatologist. Was this an appointment you knew about beforehand?"

"Yes," Mrs. Webber said. "He was diagnosed with primary sclerosing cholangitis about seven months ago. He's been ill a lot ever since and finally got on a transplant list about two months ago."

"I'm sorry, but I have no idea what that is," Rachel said.

"Few people do," Jade said.

"It's a condition of the liver where the bile ducts get clogged up," Mrs. Webber added. "And when those bile ducts get clogged, it wreaks havoc on liver cells. With Bruce's it was leading toward liver failure without a viable transplant. The appointment was essentially for a checkup to see how he was doing."

Jack, looking over toward the pot of stew-in-the making, asked, "How likely was it that he was going to get the transplant?"

"From what the specialist told us, it was looking good."

"But Dad was hesitant to hope," Tommy said. "He was very much ingrained in the worst-case scenario of things. He was fully expecting not to be around much longer."

"So in his current state, before receiving a transplant, was he considered terminal?" Rachel asked.

"Yes," Mrs. Webber said. It was the first time she seemed to be on the verge of weeping since they'd arrived.

"Had he experienced any problems with this specialist?" Jack asked.

"Not at all. Bruce had been seeing him for a little over a year and always spoke highly of him."

"Forgive the crude question," Rachel said, "but can you think of anyone that may have had something against Mr. Webber? Anyone that might have wanted to see him hurt?"

"The cops asked the same thing," Tommy said.

"And we couldn't come up with anyone," Mrs. Webber said. "Even now, two days later, I can think of absolutely no one."

"What about the few days leading up to his death?" Jack said. "Did you notice him behaving strangely? Anything that may have raised some red flags?"

Jade and Mrs. Webber both shared a look and shook their heads. "If he was acting out of character, I never noticed a thing," Mrs. Webber said.

"By any chance does the name Maria Ramirez mean anything to you?" Rachel asked.

All three of the Webbers thought about this for a moment. One by one, they shook their heads. "I can't say that it does," Mrs. Webber said. "I suppose it could have been someone Bruce worked with, but he didn't talk about work that often."

"And he hadn't worked in about five months anyway," Jade added. "He was having too many issues with his health, his liver; it just got to the point where it made no sense for him to keep going in."

Rachel considered this, her eyes locking on the cutting board, the carrots, the knife. She thought about a man that had been considered terminal, pretty much expecting the worst to happen to him, even when he was placed on a transplant list. And though she hated herself for thinking such a thing, she could not help but wonder what her current situation might be like if a transplant could save her.

She did her best to remain a part of the conversation as it went on for another five minutes, but her mind seemed hung up on that. And God help her, she could not escape from the feeling that it simply did not seem fair. It was a dark and brooding sort of selfishness and while it made her feel almost less than human, she had to accept that, along with her diagnosis, it was now a part of her.

To push it aside, she started thinking of their next steps. She knew it had to be the husband of Maria Ramirez. And even though Stanhope had warned he was likely going to be difficult, that was fine. It was Rachel's experience that once the difficult ones were made to see they weren't as special or as tough as they thought they were, they often gave the best information.

CHAPTER SIX

Rachel did her best to shrug off that overwhelming feeling of selfishness as they made the drive from the Webber house to Frank Ramirez's workplace. They'd called ahead based on Deputy Stanhope's description of the husband and were glad they did; instead of wasting about an hour heading to his home to find out he wasn't there, they knew at once that he was at work, at a construction site in a neighborhood that was less than ten minutes away from the Webber Home.

Frank Ramirez worked for a window company, and the receptionist was able to give them the address of the house he was working on. When they arrived on site, it appeared that the window company and a small crew working on the back deck of the new home were the only people on site. The home was going up on a corner lot of a well-to-do neighborhood, all homes landing in the mid-six-figures. They parked behind a beaten-up old work truck and crossed the expanse of dirt that would be a grass-filled yard soon. Rachel could already see where someone had come through to trench out the lines for a sprinkler system.

There were two men currently inside the house, visible through the still-empty window frames. Both men saw the agents approaching and it was easy to figure out which one was Frank Ramirez. He looked surprises and then annoyed. And though it was clear he knew they were there to see him, he continued working. Rachel took the lead, walking directly up to the window frame and peering into the house.

"Mr. Frank Ramirez?"

Frank was peeling a protective cover off of a pane of glass, looking up as if he'd not seen them approaching. "Yeah, that's me."

Jack beat her to the punch on showing the badge this time. "Agents Rivers and Gift, FBI. We'd like to ask you a few questions."

The look of frustration on his face backed up the little bit Deputy Stanhope had told them. Apparently, this was a failed marriage that had no hope of being repaired. "I'm sort of working here," he said.

"Yes, we are, too," Rachel snapped back. "We'll keep it short. I assume you know why we're here?"

Frank sighed and stepped away from the window. He came walking out of the front door (which did currently have a door installed) and met them where the freshly leveled sidewalk ran up to the brick stoop. Frank looked a bit smaller when he was closer to them standing out in the light of day. He looked as if he hadn't slept well in the last few days, looking to the agents as if he might zone out at any moment.

"This is about Maria, right?" Frank said.

"Yes."

"You know who did it?" he asked as if he might actually care but that the news would not really affect his day all that much.

"No," Rachel said, getting extremely irritated with his I-don't-give-a-damn attitude. "That's why we'd like to talk to you. I assume the police spoke with you?"

"They did. They told me what happened and asked lots of questions. But apparently, they did nothing with my answers if you're here. I mean, how many times do I need to be questioned?"

"Mr. Ramirez, you have a son with Maria, correct?" Jack asked. Rachel could tell that he was also getting annoyed by Frank's attitude.

"I do."

"And where is he right now?"

Frank narrowed his eyes at them, as if trying to understand why they were asking these questions. "He's with my mother."

"Here in town?"

"Yes. But what does that have to do with anything? You planning on questioning him, too? Because honestly, I'd really rather he not have to go through that."

"Just making sure we have our facts right," Jack said. Rachel was started to grow a little worried. She didn't know how much more Jack would be able to tolerate before he snapped. She'd only see it once before, and it was not pretty.

"Mr. Ramirez," Rachel said, "do you happen to know why Maria had an appointment at the hospital?"

"No. Maria and I did not talk. The only time we ever spoke is when we needed to figure out who was keeping our son. We hadn't shared anything about our personal lives together for a few years now."

"I take it the marriage ended on bad terms?"

"Yes. We were married for seven years, and it never really gelled. We only married because she got pregnant. I don't say that to be cruel. She would tell you the same thing if she were here. We were just trying to do the right thing, you know?"

"Can you think of any friends she had that might know why she went to the hospital two days ago?" Jack asked.

"No. Again, we never spoke. Any friends of hers either hate my guts or are new friends and I've never met them." He looked at them sternly, as if to make sure they'd heard him clearly. He placed his hands on his hips and looked to the ground. "Look, I'm sorry. But I really can't help you here. I hate that my son is going to have to grow up without a mother, but that's about as deeply as this bothers me. You can think I'm a selfish asshole if you want, but that's the plain and simple truth. We just didn't like one another. I'm not the right place to try getting information about Maria."

Rachel respected his blunt honesty but still wished she weren't an FBI agent so she could slap him. "What about your mother? If she's keeping your son, could she—"

"She met Maria twice and they haven't spoken in over four years. So, no. She won't be a good resource, either. You're welcome to go speak to her, but she'll be about as much help as I have been." He finally looked back up to them and asked, "Is there anything else? Can I get back to work yet?"

"Yeah, that's fine," Jack said. "Thanks for your time." The sarcasm in his tone of voice was thick.

Rachel watched as Frank Ramirez disappeared back inside the new house. Just based on the way he spoke about his ex-wife she didn't doubt anything he said but she also could not help wondering if he may be hiding something. Or if he might even be a suspect.

"Thoughts?" Jack asked when they were back in the car.

"Other than how I think Frank Ramirez is a douchebag?"

"Yes, other than that."

She cranked the car and thought about it for a moment. "We don't know why Maria was visiting the doctor yet, but we do know she and Bruce Webber *did* both have appointments with some form of doctor, *and* that they were both killed by stabbing. It makes me wonder if the coroner might be able to point us toward some more similarities. At least until we have access to Maria's medical records."

"To the coroner's office, then," Jack said, already pulling up the directions on his phone.

Rachel pulled out of the construction site, feeling rather polarized about their run-in with Frank Ramirez. It felt too harsh, too *real*—and it made her wonder if, after she was gone, Peter would have that same sort of animosity towards her.

***

In Rachel's experience, coroners seemed to come in one of two forms: the sort that was a little too into their jobs and approached it with an intense sort of morbidity or the kind that seemed bored and almost passive about the dead bodies they saw on a daily basis. The one they met half an hour after leaving the construction site was the latter. His name was Pritchard, and he had the look of a stereotypical, dry chemistry teacher. His expression was flat which, on his rather chubby face, made him look almost like a frog. It was an image Rachel could not knock out of her head as they spoke with him.

When he led them to the bodies of Maria Ramirez and Bruce Webber, he did so as if he were simply showing off some everyday items at his house—an old serving tray, perhaps, or an expensive painting. He held the notes and records of both in his hands but seemed to have already memorized the details.

"As you can see, Webber caught the worst of it," Pritchard said. Again, his delivery was deadpan. He may as well have been talking about someone getting a bad case of allergies. He went through the gamut of details as Rachel and Jack looked over the body. It was in one of the long lab drawers installed into the wall. Pritchard had taken the liberty of rolling Maria Ramirez's body—fresher and not yet placed into storage—in for a side-by-side comparison. The wounds had been mended and closed up, but it was still gruesome.

"I can't be one hundred percent certain," Pritchard said, "but I believe the first wound was the one you see there along his left side. The blade went in and down at an angle, puncturing the large intestine. From there, I believe the killer worked their way up. The wound that looks nearly vertical would be the next likely one, then the shoulder. And then, of course, the neck. It *could* all be the other way around.

"Also, one more interesting thing is that I believe the one that punctured the large intestine was the first one. But it is also the most shallow; it was not given with quite as much force as the others. The leads me to believe that either Mr. Webber saw the killer coming and jumped back, avoiding a deeper attack, or the killer was hesitant at first and then worked his nerve up with the other attacks."

Rachel agreed with this line of thought, but she also knew that there were times when killers became so enraptured in what they were doing, that they didn't pay attention to things like this—especially people that had never killed before. And because Maria Ramirez had not received the same sort of mauling, Rachel couldn't help but wonder if Bruce

31

Webber had indeed been the killer's first victim ever. If that was the case, the hesitant looking first stab wound certainly made sense.

"I have the phots from before the wounds were closed up, if you'd like to see them," Pritchard commented.

"Is there anything in them that would warrant us looking at them?" Jack asked.

"Not really. There's just visual evidence that Webber's throat was cut much worse than Mrs. Ramirez's."

"How much worse?" Rachel asked.

"Well, if you take a look at the wound across Mrs. Ramirez's throat, it looks almost harmless at first glance. This tells me the killer may have accidentally stabbed her in the stomach because the cut to the neck is so clean and direct. He did his business and left the scene. With Mr. Webber, though, it almost looked as if the killer may have been trying to saw his head off. It was quite brutal; you can even see that with the wounds closed up."

It was true. Even with Pritchard's top-notch work, it was clear to see that there were at least four distinct cut marks, none of which were as seamless and as neat as the one that had taken Maria's life. To do such brutal work in the parking lot of a specialist's office in broad daylight…it must have taken some courage. That, or the killer had simply been *that* desperate to get the murder done.

"I don't see full Y-incisions on either of them," Rachel said. "Can I assume a full autopsy was not done on either of them?"

"That's correct. At the risk of sounding heartless, I thought it was quite apparent what killed them. Also, the family of Mr. Webber said not to bother. I got no word at all from any relatives of Mrs. Ramirez."

Rachel almost asked to see the pictures Pritchard had indicated but didn't think she needed to. Even the closed wounds told the story pretty well. Rachel assumed one of two things had happened. Either the killer had just lost track of himself, slipping into some sort of fugue state when he killed Webber, or the killer had something personal against Webber which accounted for the brutal way in which he'd been killed.

It was nothing solid, but it at least gave them something more to go on.

"Thank you, Mr. Pritchard," she said. She looked to Jack and raised an eyebrow, asking: *You got anything else?*

Jack shook his head as Rachel took one last look at the bodies. Two people stabbed, the icing on the cake being slits across the throat. Both bodies killed in the parking lots of medical centers. There had to be a reason, a *link* to it all. She did her best to come up with something as she and Jack left the coroner's office, but there was nothing that stood out. She assumed Bruce Webber's bad liver might somehow be the key that—

A headache came swirling out of nowhere, blowing through her head like a hurricane. It was so sudden and sharp that it not only took her breath away but caused her to stagger backwards a bit.

Her mind instantly took her back to that morning out on the training course, how she'd been so intent to beat her record only to suffer the blackout that would cause her to go to the doctor. For a sickening moment, she *felt* like she was there, expecting the instructor and time keeper to be standing beside her.

Rachel took a deep breath and stood motionless. The pain thrummed in her head a bit but then passed away like an echo. Rachel winced against the pain and carried on, relieved to see that it started to fade even as she started to walk again. But it had been just enough to scare her—to remind her that while she was trying to find answers for these dead people, her own life was hanging in the balance as well.

Jack, already halfway across the parking lot, didn't seem to notice. And that was just fine with Rachel. She knew she could not keep it a secret from him for much longer, but she was sure as hell going to milk every moment she could before it had to come out.

CHAPTER SEVEN

Jack had noticed Rachel's brief pause as they'd come out of the coroner's office. It had lasted no more than two seconds and he'd only caught the briefest glimpse of her discomfort from a glance over his shoulder. He nearly asked if she was okay, but his concern for her had caused far too many arguments over the past few weeks. He figured if there was something truly wrong with her, she'd tell him.

Or so he hoped. He knew something was going on with her, but she wasn't opening up about it. Maybe something at home, maybe with Peter. Jack had met Peter several times and though he seemed like a good enough guy, there had been something a little stand-offish about him as far as Jack was concerned.

"Hey, Jack?" Rachel said as they came to the car. "Do you mind driving?"

"No problem."

She tossed the keys to him, and he snatched them out of the air. It seemed like a very small and unimportant moment, but Jack saw this as odd, too. Rachel sometimes insisted on driving, and it was a rarity indeed when she asked him to drive. It was such an oddity that he figured it was a pretty good opening to be able to ask if she was okay without getting his head bitten off.

"Letting me drive…you okay? Is the apocalypse upon us?"

"No," she said, feigning a smile. "Just a bit of a headache."

He nodded, not sure if he bought it or not. Regardless, he got behind the wheel and started the engine. He looked over to her and saw that she still looked uncomfortable. Something was distracting her; something had been distracting her for a while now, and she was keeping it from him.

But he wasn't going to drag it up. He'd learned his lesson over the past few weeks. So instead of asking her about it, he kept the conversation on the case. "You know, I had a thought when we were in there with the coroner. He mentioned Mr. Webber's family not requesting an autopsy. It makes me wonder…I know we're waiting for all the red tape to be cut through in order to get the medical records for both victims, but if the Webber family is willing to hand over what they know, that's permissible."

"That's right," she said, already pulling out her phone. He noticed that she waited a few minutes before making the call, as if steadying herself. "I'll see if Eloise Webber would be agreeable to that."

She made the call and placed it on speaker mode. It rang three times before it was answered by Tommy Webber.

"Tommy, it's Agent Gift again. So sorry to bother you so soon after having already left. But we were wondering about a few details of your father's medical history. I'm sure you know that the doctors won't give us medical records until the warrant clears, but even some very miniscule information would be a big help at this point."

"Well, Mom is meeting with some folks at the funeral home about coffins…," his voice hitched on the word *coffin* but he cleared his throat and did his best to forge on. "But I think I can help if it's just small stuff."

"Do you happen to know the name of the doctor your father was seeing?"

"Dr. Ailsworth was the one he saw for his check-ups. I know that much for sure. There were others here and there, but I think he was the main one."

"Was he a specialist?"

"I'm not sure. Hold on a second…I'm looking through this folder of his stuff that Mom had laying out." There was the sound of rummaging from the other end of the phone. They listened to it patiently while remaining parked in the coroner's parking lot. Jack tried to get a gauge on Rachel's condition. Whatever had been bothering her earlier still seemed to be there, but it was either fading away or she was hiding it well. He wondered if it was a physical pain or an emotional one. She hadn't mentioned her grandmother's condition much since they'd joined up. Maybe that was it.

"Okay," Tommy finally said "I've got a whole list of doctors and nurses. And most of them seem to be all at the same place, the same hospital Dad was going to regularly."

"Is that the hospital he was at on the day he—"

"Yes," Tommy interrupted quickly, not wanting to hear the end of the question.

"You said 'most of them,'" Rachel said. "Are there doctors listed there that aren't in that same hospital."

"Yeah, just one. I've got a specialist. Dr. Fenton, at Harbour Medical Group."

"Fenton?" Jack asked. It sounded familiar. It took a few seconds for it to click but he then remembered Deputy Stanhope filling them in at the scene of Maria Ramirez's murder. She'd been visiting with a specialist named Dr. Fenton.

He and Rachel shared a knowing look, coming to the same conclusion at the same time. Both victims had visited Dr. Fenton, likely meaning that Maria Ramirez also had some sort of liver problem.

"Do you have any dates?" Rachel asked. "Can you see the last time your father visited Dr. Fenton?"

"Um…hold on, hold on…yeah. Two months ago. I think it might have been about the transplant list but I'm not sure. Mom's notes aren't exactly the clearest thing."

"Tommy, this may turn out to be a huge help," Rachel said. "Thanks so much."

"Absolutely. I want this solved just as much as anyone."

"We'll be in touch," Rachel said, and then ended the call.

And then, in a complete role reversal, she pulled up the directions to Harbour Medical Group—the place where Maria Ramirez had died—to make a second visit. And now with the name of a doctor to speak with, Jack sped as he followed the robotic voice. He kept an eye on Rachel when he could. She was still wincing, still gazing out of the window or at her phone as if her mind might be somewhere else.

For perhaps the first time since he'd known Rachel, Jack found that he was starting to truly worry about her—but had no idea what he could do to help.

CHAPTER EIGHT

Rachel was rather surprised at the simplicity of the parking lot when they reached Harbour Medical Group. It was a basic rectangular shape that offered no real hiding spots for anyone trying to sneak around. For a killer to have attacked Bruce Webber in such an open space, they would have had to have been confident and reckless. That, or they'd scoped the place out very well for a few days beforehand. It offered up a creepy feeling as Jack parked in front of the building. It was a modern-looking place, the windows and edges sleek, the paintjob a blend of whites, grays, and soft blues.

Rachel's headache had all but disappeared, but the memory of it still had her reeling. Between stepping out of the coroner's office to the moment Jack parked in the Harbour lot, she'd been waiting for those little white rockets of light to go blazing across her field of vision. Thankfully, that never happened but it reminded her that no matter how hard she tried, she could not outrun it—any of it. Her marriage was ending, she had a serial killer somehow contacting people on the outside to torment her family; oh, and she was also slowly being killed by a tumor that was lurking in her brain. These were not the sorts of things you simply ran away from.

Plus, she thought as they entered the front doors of Harbour Medical Group, *if I'd been driving when that happened, the outcome could have been terrible. It could have hurt not only me, but Jack as well...and all because I'm keeping him in the dark about my diagnosis.*

It made her feel guilty, but she knew she couldn't tell Jack. Even if she had a huge change of heart and felt that it was hert responsibility to tell him, there was no way she could bring herself to do it...not after the way Peter had responded. What if Jack responded in the same way? As cliché as it sounded, Jack and her job were the only thing keeping her afloat right now. She couldn't lose him, too.

She wiped it all out of her mind as they approached the reception desk. There was a very petite blonde woman up front, no older than thirty, so Jack took the lead on it. Rachel listened as he introduced themselves and asked to speak to Dr. Fenton, but it all sounded far away, from some great distance.

"You're in luck," the cute receptionist said. "Dr. Fenton took a few hours today to prepare for a lecture he's giving in D.C. in a few weeks. He should be in his office." She paged Fenton, waited a beat and then spoke into the phone. "Dr. Fenton, there are two FBI agents here to speak with you….yes…yes, sir, I'm sure….okay."

When she looked back up to them, Rachel wondered if the young woman thought they were still *in luck*. She pointed to her right and said, "Take the elevator to the second floor. Dr. Fenton's office is the third on the left."

They walked to the elevator and as they waited for it to come down, Rachel felt Jack's eyes on her.

"What?"

"How's the headache?" he asked.

The elevator arrived, the doors slid open, and they stepped on. "Much better," she said, still feeling guilty. "It just sort of came out of nowhere. One of those things, you know?"

He nodded and though it was clear he wanted to say something else, he remained quiet. The silence remained between them until the elevator came to a stop and they both stepped out. They came to Fenton's office and knocked on the closed door.

"Come in," replied a soft-spoken voice from the other side.

Jack opened the door and they stepped inside to find a man of about fifty or so sitting behind a large oak desk. He was parked in front of a laptop and had several thick folders and binders stacked to his right. His graying hair was slicked back in a way that made him look a bit younger than he probably was.

"Agents," he said. "I feel quite sure I know why you're here but I'm afraid I'll be of little help."

"Well, we are happy for any help we can get," Rachel said. "I'm sure the police told you about Bruce Webber being murdered out in the parking lot, correct?"

"Yes. Such a terrible, terrible tragedy. As I'm sure you likely know, he'd just had success being placed on a transplant list."

"Is that what the appointment was for?" Jack asked.

"Among other things. Mr. Webber's situation was becoming rather dire, so I was wanting to keep a check on him as often as possible. Quite frankly, it was getting to the point where I was thinking of passing him on to a colleague of mine that has a very good success rate with cases that are reaching the terminal point."

"There's one more thing we're curious about," Jack said. "You recently gave a consult to a woman name Maria Ramirez. Does that name sound familiar to you?"

"It does," he said. He seemed a bit more interested now, as if he could tell things were about to take an odd turn.

"And while we know you can't give out specific medical information, can you at least tell us the outcome? Did you send her somewhere else?"

"Yes. I sent her to Dr. Ailsworth over at the hospital. Her case, while rather alarming, hadn't reached a place where I would have been able to help her just yet. I believed Dr. Ailsworth would have potentially been able to treat her so that she may not even have needed my services."

"Dr. Fenton, did you know that Maria was also killed?"

"What?" he asked, his eyes wide with shock, his mouth curling into a disbelieving frown. "When?"

The reaction seemed genuine. The shock was apparent in his eyes and his mouth seemed to be struggling on the right expression to land on.

"The day before yesterday," Rachel said. "She was coming out of the hospital, but we don't quite know why. Getting information from her family has been pretty much impossible. However, we do know now, because of what you've just said, that both she and Bruce Webber were seeing not only you, but Ailsworth as well."

"This is…I don't understand."

"We clearly don't either," Rachel said. "But as of right now, all we know is that they had doctors in common, and apparently liver issues."

"Is there any chance it's a coincidence?" Fenton asked.

"You learn pretty quickly in our line of work that coincidences aren't really a thing," Jack said.

"Dr. Fenton, do you recall the mood Mr. Webber was in the last time you saw him?"

"Not specifically," he said, clearly doing his best to think back. His eyes were wandering about the room, his hands clasped in front of him. "I mean, Mr. Webber was always sort of upbeat, despite his diagnosis. Always cracking jokes and doing his best to smile. I don't recall anything different about the last time I saw him."

"And was the one consult the only time you ever saw Maria Ramirez?"

"Yes."

"And you said you didn't see her case as quite bad enough to require a specialist, right?"

"Yes. At worst, I thought she may have a case of fatty liver disease. It's still a rather serious condition if not treated correctly, but Dr. Ailsworth would have been her best bet. If it progressed even worse, she would have likely come back to me. It's happened many times in the past, where a liver issue presents itself as something rather harmless, so I send the patient elsewhere only to have them come back to me several months later if the issue has gotten worse."

"Do you not have security cameras outside?" Jack asked.

"We only have them in the back, where the deliveries of medical supplies are made. There isn't one out front—nothing that covers the parking lot. Though, I suppose that's something to change as soon as possible."

"Would you mind if we spoke to your staff on our way out?" Rachel asked.

"Of course not. Help yourself. And please…let me know if there is anything else I can do."

"There's currently a request for medical record access," Rachel asked. "Given the diagnosis of each patient, do you think those records might be worth looking into?"

"I honestly don't know. I wouldn't think so. I just don't know why anyone would target people based on liver maladies. It seems odd."

"You're not wrong about that," Rachel said as she and Jack took their leave. "Thanks again, Dr. Fenton."

They exited his office, Jack pulling the door closed behind him. After taking a few steps away from the office, Jack peered down the hall, putting his hands on his hips. "I don't think we're going to find anything. If the police already came through here and found nothing…"

"Yeah, but we have to at least try."

"Oh, I know. But I had to go ahead and get the negativity out. What did you think of Fenton? Think he was really that shocked?"

"Yeah. He looked taken off guard for sure."

"A killer that targets folks for their livers," Jack said with a sigh. "Sounds likes some weird new kind of vampire."

"Don't joke," Rachel said. "Someone going after people with this specific sort of trait might turn out to be worse than a vampire."

She meant it as a joke, but as they started walking down the quiet hallway to start speaking with the staff of Harbour Medical Group, she couldn't suppress the light chill that crept along her spine.

CHAPTER NINE

It was his lunch break, and he spent it the same way he'd spent every lunch break for the past six years. He went to the breakroom fridge, took out the leftovers from last night's dinner, nuked them in the microwave, and took it out to his car. He hated where he worked—a small call center for consumer complaints regarding three different brands of furniture—as well as the people he worked with. So the twenty-five minutes he spent in his car, alone, was often the best part of his day.

Sometimes he listened to podcasts, and during Christmastime, he'd listen to Christmas songs on the local pop radio station. Sometimes it was YouTube videos on his phone, or doom-scrolling various newsfeeds. This was the only true alone time he had. If he wasn't working, he was trying to care for someone else. He was trying to keep someone happy…and it was a very draining process. So every now and then, a good podcast with a few twists or bits of knowledge that were new to him served as the brighter parts of his week.

But lately, over the past month or so, he'd done none of that. He's scarfed down his leftovers—usually a simple pasta dish of some kind or, on a Monday, leftover burgers or steaks he'd grilled over the weekend—and simply sat in his car in absolute silence. Sometimes he'd stare out of the windshield to the parking lot and the small strip of grass that separated it from the highway. Other times, he'd slightly recline the passenger seat and lay back with his eyes closed. He'd do one of these things and listen closely for a prompting.

It was not meditation, not really, but more of a relaxation technique that allowed him to see past the chaotic mess of his own thoughts. And lurking behind those thoughts was a very clear voice.

It was *her* voice. A voice he knew well, the voice of the one he tried so very hard to keep happy. It was a voice that he could not escape, nor did he want to. It was hard and direct, but there was love in it as well. A hard sort of love that he'd taken to heart and let mold him. He'd felt it through the years, and it had shaped the person he currently was; but now that he was an adult, the voice, like himself, had been hardened and cracked by the world. The voice had once been so sing-song and perfect but there were barbs and cracks in it now.

41

How much longer? the voice was telling him as he looked blankly out of the window. *How many more times are you going to mess this up? You think we have forever?*

He closed his eyes against her voice. It was sweet like music but also made him feel worthless. It rattled through his head like wind through dead leaves and made him think of the conversation he'd had with the gentleman in front of Harbour Medical Group. He ran it through his head like a scene from a movie he'd seen dozens of times, trying to figure out where he'd gone wrong.

"Sir, excuse me, but you have to help me."

"What is it? Are you okay?"

"You need to come with me. I can explain better when you see...I just need you to come."

He reached out to touch the man, but the man jerked away. It wasn't that motion of disgust that made him pull out the knife—no, it was the way the man had looked at him. His eyes leered and his mouth tightened in disgust.

"Get away from me. I'll call the pol—"

He'd stabbed the man before he knew it. His goal had been just one hard swipe across the neck, but some unexpected force had overtaken him. He'd barely even been in control of himself when the knife started moving. The first stab had felt like nothing more than play-acting, like he was a kid with a stick, playing the role of wanna-be ninja. But once he knew he'd pierced the skin and everything had actually *started*, it had been easier. Something dark and lively had come over him and before he knew it, the man was dead in the parking lot.

After the man had died, he'd gotten back into his car, the knife still dripping blood, the man's blood on his hands. It was the same car he currently sat in, waiting for his lunchbreak to be over so he could go back inside to this stupid, pointless job.

After killing the man, he'd heard her voice for the better part of two hours, filling his head with screams one minute and whispers of encouragement the next.

It had been with him for months now—the voice he could not escape. She filled his head as he woke up on most mornings and would speak up here and there throughout the day. It was especially interesting when she wanted to talk when he was on a call at work. It was an odd situation because he knew what she wanted, and he was willing to do it for her. But he also did not want her to go away for good this time. And he feared that if he did what she was asking—if he could actually carry it out to the end—she'd leave.

But for now, she was talking, and he listened as attentively as he could manage.

We don't have much time, she said. *We don't have much time, so I need you to listen closely. I need you to think of our time together and what you owe me. I need you to recall all those times you were never able to be quite enough—to be the man you needed to be. You can make up for all of that now. You can be a new thing, a new person altogether. You just need to listen closely and do exactly what I tell you to do.*

And then she told him what he must do. He listened closely and focused on the sound of her voice until the alarm on his phone beeped, telling him his break was over and he needed to go back to work.

CHAPTER TEN

Rachel wasn't at all surprised when they found out that Jack had called it exactly right; after an hour or so of speaking with other staff and employees of Harbour Medical Group, they came to a dead end. The only worthwhile conversation was with the woman that had first gone out into the parking lot to see the body—to make sure the patient that was leaving wasn't just over-exaggerating.

The woman's name was Eloise, and she seemed to try very hard to do a good job at recounting what she'd seen. She did not grow emotional, and she did not exaggerate or sensationalize anything. She sat with them in a small employee lounge with the same sort of candor one might show during a job interview.

"The poor woman that found the body was a lady named Peggy Windham. When she came in to tell us what she'd seen, I thought she was going to throw up right there in the front lobby. But we got her to a chair, got her some water, and she seemed to calm down."

"When she came in," Rachel said, "what did she claim to have seen? Was it just Mr. Webber's body, or did she see anything at all out of place?"

"Just the body. When the police came, they questioned her about that very same thing. She saw nothing else. They asked if she'd seen any cars leaving as she came out, but she couldn't remember."

"Okay," Jack said, his tone even and calm. "Now, you were the one that went out to confirm what she'd seen, right? You were the first other than Mrs. Windham to see the body, right?"

Yes, that's right."

"Would you be able to tell us what you saw, exactly?"

Eloise nodded grimly and straightened her back and shoulders up, as if in anticipation of the heaviness of what she was about to say. "I went straight out to where Mrs. Windham's car was parked because that's where she said she saw the body. And that's exactly where he was. We found out later that his car was right beside hers. His body had fallen in front of the cars, right between them. Some of the blood was even on Mr. Webber's bumper. I mean, at the time, it looked like it was everywhere."

"And what about you?" Rachel said. "We know Mrs. Windham claimed to have seen nothing out of the ordinary, but did you?"

"No, not a thing. I did see a single car coming in, but that was Mr. Torrence, coming in for a scheduled check-up. The cops talked to him, too, but it came to nothing. I mean, he's almost seventy and his daughter-in-law drives him to his appointments."

"Between the time you saw the body and the cops arrived, did anyone else go outside anywhere near the body?"

"No. When we called the police, they told us not to. We did have one of the male nurses stand outside to sort of stop traffic from coming in. He even wouldn't let Mr. Torrence or his daughter-in-law come out of their car until the cops arrived."

It was the most information they were able to get out of anyone at Harbour. The only real point of interest was the overwhelming amount of blood on the scene—further backing up the idea that Webber had been butchered at a much more brutal rate than Maria Ramirez.

With no clear direction from there, the most obvious place to head was the police station. Rachel supposed they could meet up with Deputy Stanhope and start looking into police records on the victims. Even this would likely be a wasted avenue, though; if Stanhope had mentioned nothing to them about records or prior charges from either of the victims, she assumed this had already been done and nothing had been found.

As Jack plugged the location of the precinct into his GPS, Rachel's phone rang in her pocket.

When she took it out and found that it was an unlisted number, she nearly ignored it. She almost *knew* who it was, alerted by some lurking sixth sense. *Right now?* she thought. *Are you serious?*

She answered the call just before she was about to pull out of the Harbour parking lot. She wasn't ready to hear his voice, wasn't ready to feel the overwhelming weight of what a conversation with him might mean.

I could be wrong, though, she thought. *It might not be him. It might be one of those scam calls where someone is going to ask me about my auto insurance…*

"This is Agent Gift," she answered.

"Your FBI friends are keeping me rather busy."

It was him. It was Alex Lynch. Somehow, he had been allowed to call her again. Even after all that had happened. She expected a surge of worry and fear but instead, there was only unbridled anger.

"Good," she hissed. "I hope they nail your ass."

"I'm quite surprised you didn't come by to visit."

"They were afraid I'd kill you with my bare hands. And believe me, I'd love nothing more. If you ever even presume to *think* about my daughter again, I'll do everything I can to make sure I can get five minutes alone in a room with you."

The tone of the conversation had grabbed Jack's attention. He had apparently already picked up on who she was talking to because he looked absolutely flummoxed. She was also glad to see that he looked a little pissed off.

"Ah, but you'd do no such thing," Lynch said. "Not if you want to know how my very sweet gift ended up in your precious daughter's room."

"Who was it?"

He chuckled and it spiked her anger even higher. "Dear, sweet Rachel. If I haven't told the barrage of idiot agents that have come to speak with me over the past three days, do you really think I'd tell you?"

"Yes, I do," she said.

"And why is that?"

"Because you like the attention. You have nothing in your life, and you want the attention. Your life is empty because I caught you and placed you in prison. And now you're trying to get back at me. I made a mistake coming to you for help. You're pathetic."

"Careful how you talk to me. Next time it might not be a dead squirrel. Next time it might be a man…a large, living man with a deplorable interest in young girls."

"Listen to me, you sick mother—"

"Sorry, Agent Gift. I believe I've been found out. Guards are coming. Bye for now."

The line went dead and when Rachel lowered the phone from her ear, her hands were trembling. She wanted to puke and scream all at once. She wanted to slam her hand through the windshield and savor the cuts and the blood.

"Rachel."

She looked to Jack and the level of worry and concern in his eyes nearly brought her to tears. Somewhere in the back of her head, she felt something that was similar to a bass drum felt from a few rooms away. It started to gently overtake most everything else in her head and she wasn't sure if it was her anger or the tumor playing some of its tricks.

"That was Lynch?" Jack asked.

She could only nod. She still felt that she might scream if she opened her mouth.

"We need to call Anderson to tell him. Someone in that prison is being lazy. That or they're giving Lynch certain advantages on purpose. Either way, someone needs to lose their job."

Again, Rachel nodded. Her fingers went to her phone to place the call herself. She started navigating to Anderson's office number when her phone rang again. She nearly dropped it in surprise but grabbed it at the last minute. This time, she saw a Roanoke area code on the caller display. This helped her to snap out of her rage-induced fugue as she answered the phone.

"This is Agent Gift."

"Agent Gift, it's Deputy Stanhope. I wanted you to know that the warrant for the medical records has cleared. I've got them emailed over here right now."

"Perfect. Would you please forward them to me when you get them?"

"Of course."

She gave him her email address and then ended the call. It was a quick and effective call, but Rachel's mind was still hung up on the call she'd just received from Lynch.

"Rachel, hold up. Before we jump back to the case, you need to address this Lynch situation. Call Anderson."

"I know!" She felt the rage trying to come out at Jack but managed to swallow it down. Lord knew she'd snapped at him more than enough over the last few weeks. He didn't deserve it, and if she planned on keeping her secret much longer, she was going to have to get better about it. "I'm afraid if I call him right now, he'll pull us off the case."

"Then he pulls us off the case. I have no spouse or kids, so I won't pretend to know what you're dealing with. But it can't be easy. Especially not with that creep still calling you."

She scrolled to Anderson's number and looked to Jack, again feeling tears welling up in her eyes. "I'm sorry, Jack."

"For what?"

For far too much, she thought. But instead of saying that—or anything, for that matter—she placed the call. Inching closer to two in the afternoon, she got what she expected. His receptionist answered, speaking with her usual, flat tone.

"Director Anderson's office."

"This is Rachel Gift I need to speak with Director Anderson, please. It's rather important."

"I'm very sorry, Agent Gift, but he's in meetings all day, and none of them are here in the office. Can I take a message?"

She didn't want to leave one but knew if she didn't, it would take far too much effort to broach the topic with him again. So she left a message, simply stating that she needed to speak with him concerning Alex Lynch, and left it at that.

Afterward, she stared through the windshield for a moment. She thought of the patrol car outside of her house and was suddenly very sure it wasn't enough. She should be home. She should be there, with Paige and Peter, even if Peter wanted nothing to do with her. To hell with this case and, for now, to hell with this job. She needed to be at home with her family.

But she knew Peter wouldn't allow it. He'd push her away, saying he couldn't trust her. He'd tell her that he didn't need her anymore and that he and Paige would be just fine without her.

The feeling gave her something of a lightbulb moment. Was that why she was refraining from telling Paige or Jack about the tumor? Was she afraid of just how quickly they'd be okay without her—of how quickly they'd come to understand that they'd be just fine when she was gone?

Before she had time to reflect on this, Jack's irritated voice broke her train of thought apart.

"To hell with that. Call the prison and speak to the warden. Speak to *someone*."

"And do you know what they'll tell me? That they need to speak with my director in order to make anything of it. So let's just wait for Anderson to call back."

He opened his mouth to argue back, but he knew she was right. He sighed and looked to her as if he wanted to hug her. "Christ, Rachel. What do you want to do now?"

"Well, the other call was from Deputy Stanhope. He's emailing me the medical records. The warrant went through."

He shook his head and looked out of the window, seemingly irritated. She almost commented on this but turned her attention to the phone. She feared if they started talking about the Lynch issue, it would open up other things. She was feeling off-balance enough as it was, and she feared that might lead to her telling him about her diagnosis.

And would that really be so bad?

She squashed the question and opened Stanhope's email as soon as it arrived. She opened the first of the PDFs and started scanning Bruce Webber's medical records. The records were from more than one place, and a compilation of the different doctors he'd seen. There were roughly thirty pages for Webber and the last page among them were the forms regarding his placement on a transplant list.

"Want me to forward this to you, too?" she asked Jack.

"May as well." Usually, she'd expect him to make a smart-ass remark. Maybe something like *I could use some light reading* or something like that. But he was still upset about the last few minutes, his tone dry and very to-the-point.

She sent Stanhope's mail to him and then opened up Maria Ramirez's file. Hers was much smaller and told the very clear story of how she had just discovered her issue about eight weeks ago. She saw where she'd initially gone to see Fenton, and then to Ailsworth. From what she could tell, the final visit to Ailsworth—the final appointment she'd ever attended in her life—had been nothing more than a back-up. Yet, the notes entered in regard to the visit stated that her condition had worsened. There were terms like *hemochromatosis* that sounded terrifying.

It was beyond eerie to think the doctor might have been making these notes while Maria had been getting murdered out in the hospital parking lot.

At the very end of her files, there was the same form she'd seen at the end of Webber's report. It was the form and paperwork for the transplant list. Based on the dates on the form, she'd been approved for the list just two weeks ago—roughly a month after Bruce Webber.

"Hey, Jack, where are you in those records right now?"

"Chapter five. It's getting a little dense."

There's the Jack I know and love, she thought. "Let me spoil the end for you. It seems Maria's case was getting worse. The same day she was killed, Dr. Ailsworth put notes in her file that she'd taken a turn for the worse. But before that, he'd also made sure she got on a transplant list. Just like Bruce Webber."

"Another connection."

"And it makes me wonder if the list might be a motive. How hard is it to get on a transplant list?"

"You're asking the wrong guy."

As theories and links started to patch themselves together, she went back to Stanhope's initial contact information and found Dr. Fenton's number. She called it and was patched through via the receptionist within twenty seconds. When Fenton answered, he sounded almost depressed. Apparently, they'd left him in quite the funk.

"Agent Gift, what can I do for you?"

"We just discovered that both Maria Ramirez and Bruce Webber were on a local list for liver transplants. How difficult would it be for us to get a copy of that?"

"Not too difficult, actually. Give me about five minutes and I'll shoot it over to you. Where do you want it sent?"

Again, she gave her email address and when she ended yet another call, she was starting to feel something almost like a groove. Call after call, bits of information coming almost at will now, and things seemed to be leading somewhere. The groove was not nearly enough to erase the reality that Alex Lynch had once again called her, but it helped to keep her mind from focusing solely on it.

The email came earlier than expected, Fenton fulfilling his end of things in under three minutes. The document was a bit underwhelming—just a list of names and addresses along with the age and current diagnosis of the listed individual. She didn't have to scan it long before she came across Bruce Webber's name.

"Webber is the seventh name from the top," she told Jack. After a bit more scanning, she found Maria's. "Maria Ramirez is the nineteenth entry."

"So the question then becomes," Jack said, "is one of the people on this list the killer?"

"Why would they be?"

"To get close to the top," Jack said, and Rachel was a little ashamed she hadn't gotten there first.

"Another question, though." And before she could even say it, the weight of what it might mean slammed into her like a brick. "Does that mean anyone higher than Webber on the list could be the next victim?"

Jack gave her a determined smile, one that may have seemed evil or malicious to people that did not know him. "I think we need to find out."

CHAPTER ELEVEN

They arrived at the Roanoke City Police Department at 2:35 and Rachel's mind was alighted with the new questions and possibilities. Deputy Stanhope met them there, just having got in from routine patrols himself. He looked hurried but slightly excited when he saw Rachel and Jack coming to his desk. He didn't have an office, but a large cubicle space where a few other officers shared the floor. A busier area that Rachel supposed served as the bullpen sat on the other side of a wall, slightly noisy. Like any other police station, she'd ever stepped foot in, there was the murmur of several conversations, the sounds of fingers dancing across keyboards, and the smell of too-strong coffee in the air.

"So I take it the docs were helpful?" Stanhope said as they huddled around his desk.

"We only spoke with Fenton," Rachel said as they came to his desk. She had her phone out, the transplant list already pulled up. "But it was your email with the records that really helped and led us to this."

She handed him her phone and he took it eagerly. "What am I looking at?" he asked.

"A transplant list for people in need of a liver. Notice that Bruce Webber is listed as seventh from the top. Maria Ramirez is a bit further down."

"We suspect the people above Webber may be potential targets for the killer," Jack said. "And that the killer may be somewhere below Webber. This is all speculation, of course."

"If that's the case," Stanhope said, "why skip so far down to Ramirez? Wouldn't it make more sense to hit someone further up?"

"If our theory is right, yes," Rachel said. "But it could have just been opportunistic. He may have simply known where Maria was going to be. This literally could be a target list and the order means nothing. Whenever he happens to come across a time and place where he can attack any of them, he takes it."

Stanhope scanned the list and chuckled. "There are four names below Ramirez. Would it be a safe bet to say one of them might be the killer?"

"It would be logical, but not *safe*," Rachel said.

51

"So what do you need from the PD?"

"I think anyone above Ramirez needs to be considered a potential target for the killer," Rachel said. "They need to be protected...warned."

"I agree, but we simply don't have that sort of manpower right now, Agent Gift. If we could weed the list down to make sure we're hitting the most relevant people, that would be a huge help. And even then, this could turn out to be a shit-show. Telling this many people they may be the target for a killer is going to open up a flood of gossip of unimaginable proportions."

"That might be a good thing," Jack pointed out. "If we try protecting those people and it gets back to the killer, maybe it will discourage him."

"Not to mention that right now, this is all we have," Rachel said. "And if we want to prioritize, I think we focus on the top six names on the list."

"I can get a few officers to call the people on the list but sending men out to routinely patrol them is a bit much to expect," Stanhope said.

"I agree," Rachel said. It instantly brought to mind the policemen that were currently parked outside of her house, making sure none of Alex Lynch's cohorts would try anything else. "First, maybe we can thin the list out by calling the doctors on the list. There are only five different doctors listed, so it won't take long. If we can rule out people based on whether they are currently hospitalized or in some other form of care, that will knock some of the names off."

"And I can check the names against the database," Stanhope said. "If any of them have criminal records, we flag them as the potential killer." He seemed anxious, like a bull wanting to surge out of the rodeo gates.

"You good to orchestrate all of that?" Rachel asked.

"I'm on it. It's a lot of work, but a lot easier than sending every unit we have out to check on upwards of twenty people."

"Where can we set up?" Rachel asked.

"I know it's not too glamorous, but there are a few empty cubicles on the other side of this wall," he said, nodding to the other side of the room where a hallway intersected it all. "I'll run by the front and let them know to make sure you have network access right away."

***

Rachel and Jack were set up with two laptops—both rather old but in perfectly fine working condition—and began tag-teaming with Stanhope and his team. Working together in such a way made Rachel feel that sense of working against a clock bearing down on them with much more force.

"You know," Jack said roughly fifteen minutes into the process. "I think what I said earlier might turn out to be the case here--about the killer potentially being scared away if the word gets out."

"It's a happy thought, sure," she said with a lighthearted smirk. "But if we don't know his motive, we can't really assume such a thing."

"Well, not only that," Jack went on, undeterred, "there's also the possibility that he *is* one of the people lower on the list. If we call him, thinking he's just one of the people on the list, *that* could also dissuade him from killing again. It might make him feel like the pressure is on and we're breathing down his neck. We could win this whole thing without even realizing it."

"That *is* a good point," Rachel said. "My fear there, though, is that it might also convince him to work faster. If he's on a transplant list— that is, if our theory is right and he's killing these people to get closer to the top of the list—he might be so desperate that he's beyond caring about his consequences."

"Jesus, Rachel, what is it with you not enjoying a peek at the bright side every now and then?"

She knew it was just a one-off joke, but it landed hard. She knew she'd missed any sort of bright side these last few weeks, given the enormity of bad news she'd been dealt. And day by day, it seemed to be getting worse: her own diagnosis, Grandma Tate's diagnosis, the drama with Lynch's dead squirrel, Peter walking out…she was almost afraid to even imagine what might come next.

She kept the question away by focusing on the multiple tasks at hand. She took it upon herself to call around to hospitals and medical care facilities to narrow down their list by removing the names of any current patients from the list. After calling every local place that fit the bill, she was able to strike only three names from the list. She did, however, also take the opportunity to leave a warning with each facility, letting them know the bare bones details of the case; she didn't come right out and tell each place that they would make ideal targets for the killer, but she thought it might be very likely.

While everyone worked in a flurry, it all seemed to go by slowly. Rachel assumed it was because they were all bogged down with the knowledge that there was an active killer out there, perhaps even planning his next attack, while they were sitting in the station behind phones. An announcement was made whenever a name was crossed from the list and within forty-five minutes, they had the list whittled down to just sixteen potential names. It was around this time, roughly forty-five minutes in, when Stanhope's voice spoke up above the din, louder than usual.

"I think I've got a hot ticket here!"

He came walking around the cubicle walls with a laptop in his hand. He set it down on the desk Rachel and Jack were using, the screen showing a plain-looking Caucasian man's mugshot. Rachel scanned the preliminary information and recognized the name right away. She had, after all, scanned over it roughly fifty times in the past hour or so.

"Daniel Robinson," Stanhope said. "Arrested twice in the past seven years: once for breaking and entering, once for assault. The assault charge involved an attempted stabbing, and he did six months in prison for it. And he just happens to be the twentieth name on the list."

Rachel was up at once, surprised to find that she felt almost guilty for leaving the local PD to run the rest of the phone-related tasks. Jack joined her, giving Stanhope a congratulatory back. "Good work, Deputy. Can you text us that address?"

"You know, I think I'd like to come with you."

Rachel and Jack shared a quick glance, not long enough to come off as rude, but long enough for Stanhope to notice.

"I know, I know," he said. "Local PD cramping your style and all that. but I know the city like the back of my hand and besides that, if this ends up being your guy, you'd need local PD presence before it's all said and done, anyway."

Rachel had never liked it when local PD tagged along but she also knew that there was a bit of logic to Stanhope coming along. Also, there was no sense in wasting time arguing about it. So Rachel put on her best cooperative smile and nodded toward the exit.

"Lead the way."

Stanhope did, and gladly. Rachel and Jack followed him out of the precinct as several officers continued to make calls behind them, making sure they trimmed down the transplant list as much as possible.

CHAPTER TWELVE

The only awkward moment in heading to the suspect's residence with Stanhope was the fact that they took his patrol car, and Jack sat in the back. Rachel couldn't help herself when she smiled glibly at him through the cross work of iron between the front and back seats. Jack responded in kind, flashing his middle finger when Stanhope has his head turned.

Rachel also found that she was quickly starting to like Stanhope quite a bit. He did not find the need to fill the awkward silence between them with useless chatter, telling them every little secret about every little street or corner they passed. She could feel the seriousness coming off of him, a cop that was focused solely on solving a case and keeping his city protected. He simply drove to the address he'd taken from Daniel Robinson's record, eyes set straight ahead and speeding along with a sense of urgency the case deserved.

He drove them into a part of town that Rachel didn't quite consider "the bad part of town" but it was just a couple of steps away. The houses were all piled in on one another, most of which were boarded up and abandoned. Empty beer bottles remained on the sidewalks from the night before and most of the lawns were either dead or entirely overgrown.

Daniel Robinson lived in a house with a yard that was somewhere in between—the grass gone mostly brown but showing signs that he at least took the time to mow it every now and then. Stanhope parked alongside the sidewalk. and they all got out. Being the middle of the day on a weekday, the street was mostly quiet, though Rachel could hear distant chatter a street or two further off.

They walked up the two old concrete stairs embedded into the yard, and then along the cracked sidewalk to the front porch. The porch was mildewed and somehow smelled like rainwater even though the yard and streets showed no signs of rain for at least the last two days. Both Rachel and Jack stood back to allow Stanhope to knock on the door. When he did, the door rattled slightly in its frame. Right away, Rachel assumed no one would answer—that Mr. Robinson might have a job that he was currently at, or that he was out and about on errands.

But the sound of shuffling footsteps could be heard through the door, coming their way. Seconds later, they could hear the sound of a lock being disengaged. The door slowly opened but only a bit. A man peered out at them, his face old and tired. Rachel assumed this might be Daniel Robinson's father.

"Yeah?" the man said. When he noticed a cop at his door, he did not change his tone, nor did he open his door any wider. "What do you need?"

"We're looking for Daniel Robinson," Stanhope said. "Is he around?"

"That's me," the man at the door said.

"With all due respect," Stanhope said, "our records indicated that Robinson is fifty-five years old."

The man at the door chuckled and the noise sounded more like a cough than anything else. "That some sort of insult?"

"I'm sorry, sir," Stanhope said. "You're Daniel Robinson?"

"That's me," he said again.

"The same Daniel Robinson that was arrested three years ago on an assault charge that involved an attempted stabbing?"

"Wish I was known for more than that, but yes. Officer, what the hell is this about?"

Rachel stepped in, showing her badge as she looked in at the man. If he was indeed Daniel Robinson, he was sick. Which made sense, considering he was on a transplant list for a liver.

"Mr. Robinson, I'm Agent Rachel Gift with the FBI, and this is my partner, Agent Rivers. We've recently learned that you're on a transplant list for a liver, correct?"

"Yeah. That a crime?"

"No, sir. We just need to know if—"

"Listen," Robinson interrupted. "You know about the liver, and you've already indicated that I look like shit. So, I'm sure you'll understand if I ask you to leave. With all due respect, I don't feel like wasting my time with the police."

He made a movement to shut the door but Rachel quickly put her foot in. She could tell by just the amount of force he put into it that he had no energy. He was sick and if he was this weakened by whatever his condition might be, she found it hard to believe that Daniel Robinson could be the killer. As she looked through the now-larger crack in the door at him, she saw that he was a sizable man, but he presented himself like someone that was about to fall over.

It did not escape her that this might be an act. Maybe he'd thought quickly enough to put on this little charade after Stanhope had mentioned the transplant list. *But you sure can't fake how old and tired he looks,* she thought. *No one is that good of an actor.*

"Sir, if we could just as you a few questions…"

"About what, exactly? I've done my time for my crimes. And if I'm being honest with you, I feel like I'm still paying for it. I didn't believe in karma but…well, you know about my liver. You know I'm on that list. You know…"

Rachel hated herself a bit for what she was about to do, but she knew it was the most surefire way to ensure Robinson was not putting on an act. She made a very quick motion forward, as if she intended to push the door open and go inside. She made it to the doorway, her hand on the door, and watched as Robinson reacted.

He was slow—almost to the point that it looked like he was frozen in place. He took a few shuffling steps back and for a sickening moment, Rachel feared he might actually fall over. She could hear Stanhope behind her, apparently coming to the same conclusion she was.

"Jesus," he whispered.

"Mr. Robinson," Rachel said, "are you actively seeing a doctor for your issues?"

"Check-ups only. Insurance isn't really cutting it much and I…I just…"

Stanhope stepped forward now, with Jack behind him. Both men looked overly compassionate, probably to try to contrast the quick and sudden movement Rachel had just used to frighten him.

"Mr. Robinson," Stanhope said, "we have reason to believe that someone out there is attacking people that are currently on that transplant list. So for the next few days, I need you to be very careful. Don't answer this door again unless it's someone you know."

"Who'd do a thing like that? Attacking sick people?"

"We don't know. We're trying to find out right now. Mr. Robinson, could you tell us where you were two afternoons ago?"

He thought about it but was clearly still pissed off. "I went with my daughter to a natural healing-type place. Just a bunch of bullshit if you ask me, but it was important to her."

"You buy anything?"

"She did, yeah. I told her not to. Got me this ointment that smells like crap."

Rachel tucked this all away as an alibi. With a potential receipt, a daughter, and the staff at the store, it would be easy enough to validate.

"Mr. Robinson, when is your next appointment?" Rachel asked.

"Tomorrow."

"How do you get there?"

"My daughter picks me up and takes me. We go get a milkshake with my granddaughter afterwards."

It was a touching gesture, as Rachel realized Stanhope was on the verge of offering the man a ride to his appointment tomorrow if he didn't already have one.

"That sounds great," Stanhope said. "We're very sorry for taking up your time. But like I said…you don't answer this door for anyone other than the police or your daughter. Okay?"

"Yeah," he said, giving Rachel an uncertain glance as he slowly started to close the door. This time, Rachel stayed out of the way and let him close the door, unhindered.

***

Stanhope took them back to the precinct and on the way back, the patrol car was again filled with silence. After the trick she'd pulled on Robinson, Rachel felt she should be the one in the back this time. She also struggled with trying not to feel that visiting Daniel Robinson had been a dead end. In reality, that's exactly what it was but the visit also allowed them to knock one more name off of the transplant list.

Just before they arrived back at the precinct, Stanhope got a call over the citizen's band radio from the dispatch desk. "Deputy Stanhope, come in would you, please?" a female voice said.

Rachel was happy to see them using a CB radio. They seemed to be going the way of the dinosaur as more and more breakthroughs came about in the cellular and mobile sectors.

"This is Stanhope, come on back."

"Wanted to you know that the Captain has approved the rounds for protection on the top five people on that transplant list. Beyond that, we just don't have the manpower. The first shifts are rolling out in about an hour."

"Yeah, I figured that would be the best we'd be able to get," Stanhope said. "Thanks, all the same."

Even though it was only five people, it was still a relief. While the killer's motives were still little more than guesswork, Rachel knew the safest bet was that he was trying to get to the top of the list for some reason or another. And now that there was a chance that he knew what they were up to (assuming he had been called or contacted in some form by the police today), that seemed even more likely than before.

Getting out of the car in the officer and patrol lot, the agents and Stanhope parted ways. Stanhope seemed hopeful they would get their man which did Rachel a world of good. She knew it was probably just another effect of her recent troubles, but she'd been easily discouraged as of late. To hear someone other than Jack trying to convince her all was well was a welcome treat.

"Something like this in a city as compact as Roanoke…I think we'll find our guy by sunrise," he said. "I'll keep a check on the patrols that are out to keep watch over the would-be victims. If you two need anything at all, don't hesitate to call."

With that said, Stanhope headed back into the precinct while Rachel and Jack made their way back over to their bureau car. Dusk wasn't on them yet, but it was making itself known in the fading light and cooler temperatures. Being closer to the mountains than Richmond, the Roanoke evening was cooler than Rachel had been expecting, reminding them that fall closer than they thought.

Before getting into the car, Rachel excused herself to the side of the parking lot where she took out her phone. She knew Paige would be at soccer practice, taken by the sitter, but she needed an update. It was started to wear on her, not being around them while there was so much uncertainty and tension in the air. But to get any sort of update, she was going to have to call Peter.

Before she handled the awkwardness of that fact, her mind was still caught up on the idea that Paige was being taken to soccer practice by her babysitter. Rachel had taken her to a few practices here and there, so she knew it was nothing unusual for some kids to have sitters or grandparents, or aunts or uncles, to take the players to practice. But she was very aware that neither she nor Peter had taken her to a practice in a while. She wondered how many practices one of them had been at. She knew there had been *zero* practices where they had both been there, and she wondered if it was one of those things Paige was noticing but choosing to push way down and not bring up out of fear of making her parents feel bad.

The guilt of this dashed any last-minute changes of heart in making the call to Peter. She pulled up his number, knowing he'd be upset that she was calling him at work. But he'd just have to suck it up and deal with it.

She didn't know what to expect when he answered the phone, so when he finally answered on the third ring, his indifferent tone did not bother her.

"Hey, Rachel."

"Hey. I just wanted to check in while I had the chance."

"Okay. I mean…we're good here. I'm at work, Paige is at school."

He was a little dryer than usual and was clearly annoyed that she had called. She hated that she felt he now had a very strange power over her, but she supposed it was her fault for not pushing a little harder to stay off of this case. If she had done the smart thing and stayed at home, she wouldn't have to rely on him for updates.

"Are the cops still parked outside of our house?" she asked.

"They were there when I left the house this morning. And one of them did tell me that the principal of the school has been informed of Paige's situation. There's also going to be a patrol car near the soccer field this evening for her soccer practice."

"How's Paige taking it all?"

"She's fine. I think she might not have even noticed the cops outside the house."

Rachel doubted this. Paige was quiet about many things, but that did not mean she wasn't observant. The girl had one of the keenest eyes Rachel had ever seen in a kid. She'd often amused herself thinking that she could already see FBI qualities in her daughter. Now, though, such a thought wasn't so amusing.

"Any idea when you'll be home?" Peter asked.

"No. We're still sort of stuck in the middle of this case."

"Okay," he said, sounding unsurprised. "Well, I'll let Paige know you called."

"And you? How are you, Peter?"

"I'm fine. Just busy." He hesitated a moment and then said, "How are you?"

She thought of the headache she'd felt trying to take her by surprise when she'd come out of Harbour Medical Center, that terrifying moment where she feared another blackout was coming. "I'm good," she said, waving the memory away. "Like I said…just wanted to check in."

"The police are still around, and Paige and I are fine. We're good. But I have to get back to work, and—"

"Yeah, I know. Thanks for taking the call."

"Sure."

The call ended abruptly. She was pretty sure it was the first time in a very long time they'd ended a call without *I love you* from at least one of them.

She looked back to the bureau car, where Jack was sitting in the passenger seat, waiting. She hated keeping this secret from him, but she also hated the idea of thinking he would treat her differently because there was a tumor in her brain. She made her was slowly to the car, making sure she had her game face on before getting back behind the wheel.

"Everything good?" he asked.

"Yeah. Just parent guilt. It's yet another soccer practice where Paige is being escorted by a sitter."

"Will there be a cruiser there watching out for her?"

"Peter says there will be, and…"

She stopped here, sure that she would start crying at any moment. She shook her head and started the car. "I can't. Not right now. I need to just wrap up this fucking case as quickly as I can so I can get back home. And I'll just have to tell Anderson I'm not working any more until this Alex Lynch situation is resolved."

She could tell he wanted to say something, that he was putting a lot of thought into whether or not he should try to go deeper. In the end, he stayed quiet. She appreciated it because she knew his nature. He *wanted* to get to the bottom her pain and why she was on the verge of getting emotional. To stomp it down showed great restraint and respect for her.

Jack pulled up a list of nearby hotels while Rachel pulled out onto the street. The drive between Roanoke and Richmond was only about two and a half hours, but it made little sense to head back home when there were active patrols keeping watch on only five out of more than a dozen potential victims. Not only that, but they hadn't really gotten much accomplished.

"I say we get a hotel, grab some dinner, and head out to see if we can help with these patrols," Jack said. "That good with you?"

"Yeah. I'll need to call to check in on Paige, too. Sorry for all the personal calls, but I think—,"

"Shut up, Gift. I'd be judging you if you *weren't* concerned. You do what you need to do. Okay?"

"Yeah," she said. She was very aware that she did not sound convincing.

"If you say so," he said. "Just let me take this opportunity to go ahead and get this out of the way for what will now be the third case in a row: if something's bothering you and you need to talk it out—"

"I know. You're all ears. You don't mind listening."

"Oh, I mind it," Jack said. "And quite frankly, I'm not very good at it. But yeah, I'm here for it."

Rachel drove a bit further away from the precinct and, neither of them being picky, chose a Sleep Inn primarily because it was in walking distance of a chain restaurant. The two of them had worked together long enough to be comfortable with the motel check-in process, getting it down to quick sort of science now. Only on one occasion had they been forced to share a room; it had been awkward and almost unbearably comical, and they swore to avoid it all costs in the future.

Keys in hand, with rooms directly beside one another, they entered their respective rooms. Rachel was feeling surprisingly fine, the major headache just a distant memory now. With the list being thinned out and what appeared to be a very odd motive on the table, she was actually feeling thrilled to be on the case. It was rare that she was involved in a case where finding the killer came down to a list and a simple process of elimination, and something seemed almost academic about it—methodical.

She entered the room and found it exactly like the countless others she'd stayed in over the years. Decently made, smelling of old shoes and a faint air freshener, everything tidy, just enough to seem in place. She kicked off her shoes and looked to the bed, wanting to simply crash and watch a bit of TV. But the case was too close to her now and she knew it was all her mind would be on.

Well, that wasn't true. She was still thinking of Alex Lynch, and of Paige. She checked her watch and saw that Paige should be getting home from soccer practice in about an hour. Maybe she'd call Paige, order some Chinese or Thai from somewhere, and invite Jack out for a beer to go over the case.

And tell him what's being going on? Maybe tell him about the little intruder in your brain that is going to kill you in about a year or so?

"Maybe," she said out loud. And even the idea of it *did* bring a bit of relief.

So then why are you so scared?

She had no answer for that. but the heaviness of it was enough to make her go ahead and sit on the edge of the bed. She put on the TV but didn't pay much attention to it. It served as nothing more than background noise as her mind spiraled in several directions: the transplant list, the victims, Alex Lynch, Paige, Peter, her tumor…

Slowly, Rachel lay back on the bed and stared at the ceiling, trying her best to sort everything out in her head. Even lying down on her back, she felt dizzy and out of control. She lay there for a very long time, barely moving, as she felt her life slowly slipping out of her control in all directions.

CHAPTER THIRTEEN

He knew what he had to do next, but it was going to be hard. Not the act of murder itself—no, he felt that with two under his belt, he was getting quite good at it. He was quite sure that he'd be able to completely control himself with the third victim. A quick and brutal act, in and out, and that would be it. There one second and gone the next.

That was the plan, anyway. But looking at the house, he wasn't sure it was going to exactly work out that way.

The hard part was going to be getting to the victim. He had no appointment to use to his advantage this time, but he did know where they lived. He'd staked the house out for about ten days or so. He knew the schedules of the family, knew when they left the house and when they arrived back home. He also knew the layout of the yard fairly well. They had one of those Ring doorbells on the front porch, so he was going to have to stick to the side of the yard and hope no nosy neighbors saw him. The yard was separated by the neighbors on both sides by a black iron fence and several trees, so he didn't think that would be an issue.

Oddly enough, the act of breaking and entering seemed to bother him more than murder. Murder, from what he'd learned so far, was quick and to the point. But it seemed to him that breaking and entering took more forethought and ambition.

He knew how he was going to do it, though. He'd been around to the back of the house once before, just a few days ago. Doing so had made him forty minutes late for work and he'd been chewed out for that, but he really didn't care. He knew the call center was having trouble keeping help so unless he went into the manager's office and pissed in his face, he doubted he was going to get fired for showing up late a few days.

Though, he supposed if it was ever found out that he'd been stalking people and then murdering them, that might cross a line, too.

He smirked at the idea as he drove by the house. Knowing it wouldn't do to just park right in front of the house, he drove a few blocks down and parked at the edge of a block where a house was currently for sale. He supposed it was inconspicuous enough. He made himself get out of the car, not wanting to allow himself a moment to change his mind. As he started walking down the street, he felt the knife pressing almost urgently against his thigh, where he had it safely planted between his hip and the waist of his pants. It both excited and terrified him to know he'd be using it soon.

Well, maybe not *soon*. His target did not get home for another three hours or so and God only knew how long it would take them to be alone. He started to wonder if this was a mistake. Hell, he didn't even know if he'd be able to get into the house at all. He'd done some research online, reading up on how to pop a window up from the outside even if it was locked. He'd need a flathead screwdriver, which he also had on him. It was a small one, tucked away in his left front pocket.

Keeping his head low, he walked down the street and was surprised at how dead and quiet the place was during the afternoon. On his trips by the house to make sure he knew the area well, he'd always seen people out jogging or walking, but there was none of that right now. Still, the nerves were there, his worry of—

My God, would you stop worrying about everything? You've always been open to question everything if it didn't make sense to you, haven't you? It's why a woman never settled down with you. It's why you didn't make it out of college and are now stuck with that God awful job that you hate. You're wasting your life away because you question everything, all the time, and never settle your mind on something unless you believe you know all aspects of a thing. You're such a rotten little disappointment, never doing anything right, never putting your all into something...

"Fuck you," he muttered. Heat flushed his face at the two words because he'd never dream of saying them to her face-to-face. Even the thought of it felt a bit taboo.

And somehow, with that, he'd come to the house. For a paralyzing moment, his legs felt as if they would refuse to carry him any further. Not into the yard, not up onto the back porch to the kitchen window, and certainly not into the house.

But he made himself, not wanting to hear the voice tear him down anymore. The knife pressed against his thigh and the shape of the little screwdriver weighed down his front pocket. He started into the yard and walked with his head down along the fence. The voice appeared again, this time giving a very rare positive comment, and that was all he needed.

There you go, baby. There you go...

He was practically sprinting when he came to the back porch stairs, slowly taking the screwdriver out of his pocket.

CHAPTER FOURTEEN

Rachel dozed off, but only for a few moments. The difference in the volume on the TV between the program that was on and the ear-shattering noise of a commercial for a local business jarred her out of her thin bit of slumber. Embarrassed that she'd fallen asleep at all, she first looked towards the blinds to make sure it wasn't pitch black outside. When she saw only the muted purple colors of the sun, she relaxed a bit as she sat up.

As the remnants of the doze wore off, she checked her watch. It was nearing 6:30, which meant Paige would be back home from soccer practice. She doubted Peter was home yet, meaning the sitter would likely be preparing something simple for dinner. She thought of calling Peter again, just to touch base with him on any talks he'd had with her about Grandma Tate or the dead-squirrel situation but decided it might be a bad idea. She didn't want to be depressed or angry when she spoke with Paige; so she called Paige first, knowing soccer practice ended half an hour ago, and wondered just how much Peter had already told the babysitter.

As was usually the case, the sitter allowed Paige to answer the phone whenever Rachel called. When she answered, she was holding a juice box in one hand—apple-cranberry flavored because that was Paige's new fixation.

"Hey, Mommy!"

"Hey, Paige. How was school?"

"It was okay. We learned about the Egyptians and the pyramids today. And I told Mrs. McCoy that Daddy one time watched a show about how some people think the pyramids were made by aliens."

"Oh, Paige…you didn't."

"It's okay. Mrs. McCoy thought it was funny."

"Have you already done all of your homework?"

"All of it. We're about to eat dinner."

"And how about soccer practice? Did that go okay?"

"Oh yeah, it was good. I scored two goals. Coach Byron thinks I'll be able to start on Saturday!"

"Hey, that's so awesome! Good job. Listen, Paige…has your Daddy called this evening?"

"He texted. He's going to be a little late, but in time to put me into bed." She paused here, sipped from her juice box, and said, "So I guess you won't be home tonight?"

"No. But you know…I'm not that far away Just two and a half hours. So when we get this thing wrapped tomorrow—hopefully—it won't take me too long to get home."

"Oh. Okay."

The harshest thing of all was that Paige truly didn't seem to mind all that much. She was used to her parents not being there. And before too long, Rachel realized, she was going to be used to her mother not being there at all.

What the hell are you doing here, working? she asked herself. She wondered if a stage of receiving devastating news was self-loathing. If so, she was quickly coming up on it.

"I'm really sorry I have to be here right now," Rachel said, hating herself even more because she wasn't sure if she meant it. When speaking to Paige, she wasn't really sure about anything.

"It's okay. We had fun at Grandma Tate's right?"

"Yeah, I'm glad you enjoyed it. You be good for Ms. Nelson, okay?"

"It's Kaitlin!" Kaitlin Nelson, one of their two go-to sitters yelled from the back.

"Need to talk with me about anything Kaitlin?"

"No ma'am! We're going to have chicken alfredo, a cupcake, and then watch a movie. And then it's bedtime."

"Thanks, Kaitlin."

"Absolutely."

"And you," she said, redirecting her attention to Paige, her face still huge and prominent in the screen. "I miss you."

"I miss you, too. Bye, Mommy!"

They ended the call and the moment it was over, Rachel decided that she was not going to call Peter for a second time. Right now, with the way things were between them, there would be no good to come of it. Instead, she took a shower and sat in front of the local evening news until Jack knocked on her door to go grab dinner.

She left the room feeling like a bad mother but with a case in front of her as a distraction. It was a wretched juggling act, but one she was getting far too good at. The trick now was deciding if it was a good or a bad thing, and she wasn't sure if it was an answer that she was ready to hear.

Rachel spent the next five minutes finding the number to a Chinese restaurant and calling in a delivery order. She then showered, dressed, and seriously considered going with her original idea of asking Jack out for a beer to talk about the case. She knew it wasn't exactly an encouraged practice, but it was Rachel's experience that deep talks over a few drinks tended to open up avenues of discussion that may not be breached in car rides, offices, or stuffy conference rooms.

But as she waited for her food to arrive, she wondered if such an outing would be the best move. Outside of typical work barriers, Jack tended to be a little friendlier than he did when they were "on the clock." She doubted he'd have as much of a problem really trying to dig into what had been bothering her lately. She'd noticed that so far on this case, he'd kept it to a minimum—likely because she'd nearly bitten his head off a few times ever since receiving her diagnosis.

So maybe going out for a drink was a bad idea. She thought it over while she sat at the small table, looking at the tidy pile of notes and files they'd accumulated so far on the case. She kept going back to the transplant list, finding that it was indeed an odd sort of hit list. More than that, she found herself thinking of the kind of emotions that must go through someone after putting their name on such a list. Was it more anticipation or dread? Did your name going on the list instantly create a sense of relief or was there just one more thing to worry about?

As she considered all of this, she inserted her own situation into it. She wondered what her life might be like if she came clean with *everyone* and then called up her doctor to see what her first steps might be in terms of trying to beat this. She knew her chances were incredibly slim…but *what if?*

It struck her then, not for the first time, that maybe her refusal to seek treatment was selfish. If she hated the idea of Paige growing up without a mother, then shouldn't she at least *try* to make sure that didn't happen? And if she did reach out to a doctor, if she did decide to start options like chemo, would it illicit hope or fear?

She didn't know, though it was the first time she'd allowed herself to openly think about such things. She knew if she came clean with everyone and sought treatment, her career would essentially be over. Every waking minute of her life would be dedicated to retiring and working towards trying to beat the cancer. But if it was a battle that she knew she had a small chance of beating, why even take the punishment? Why put Paige through watching her mother slowly deteriorate and waste away, sick all of the time, with no real—

A knock on the door broke her out of her thoughts. She came out of them with a jerk, almost the same way she'd been pulled form her impromptu nap earlier. She'd nearly forgotten about the Chinese food.

She took the food, paid and gave a tip, and then sat on the edge of the bed. Any thought of calling Jack to head out for a drink had been dashed by the inner dialogue she'd just had with herself. She suddenly didn't feel like seeing Jack. Hell, she didn't even feel like leaving this motel room and venturing outside. She simply sat on the edge of her bed, the TV blaring its nonsense, and ate her orange chicken. On occasion, she'd look over to the table, her eyes searching out the transplant list as if she was sure there was an answer there somewhere—not just to the case, but to her own turmoil as well.

CHAPTER FIFTEEN

Christina Ragland looked through the blinds of the living room window and easily spotted the cop car parked on the side of the street. The shape of it was perfectly outlined in a nearby streetlight. According to the call she'd received from the police roughly three and a half hours ago, there were two men in the car—and they were there to make sure she was not attacked by some maniacal killer that was taking people out seemingly because they were on a transplant list.

Running it over in her head, it sounded pretty ridiculous. It was almost like the punchline to a morbidly dark joke. It was bad enough having a liver that had decided to simply stop working properly seven months ago and ensuring the endless doctors' visits that came with it, but now she could very well be killed because of it…and it would have nothing to do with her bad liver.

"You're going to drive yourself crazy if you keep looking out there."

She turned away from the window to the couch where her husband was watching television. He was watching one of those shows where Gordon Ramsay was yelling at people. The comment was not made out of irritation, but out of concern. As a matter of fact, Ryan seemed to have taken the news harder than Christina had when the call had come in. He'd already gone to the upstairs coat closet to retrieve the Smith and Wesson he'd owned for three years and only ever used once, at a target range. It was currently with them in the living room, wedged between the cushion at the end of the couch and the armrest because it made Christina very uneasy to see it out in the open.

"I'm just checking," she said, joining him on the couch.

'The cops will handle it," Ryan said. "I bet you anything they'll have this whacko before the morning even gets here."

Christina actually felt the same. The situation itself felt too absurd to be taken seriously—the sort of thing she might read about online or in a friend's odd Facebook post. Also, with so many cops out and about to protect her and several others, surely there was an equal amount of manpower being used to find the killer. And though she felt this rather strongly, the fear was still there. To know there was a killer out there that had read her name on a list and may *eventually* make his way to

71

her was unnerving. She supposed that was why she was starting to almost feel numb to it. It was the same feeling of danger she supposed some people got when walking by a hornet's nest. You knew the hornets were there and would sting you if you got too close, but as long as you kept your distance, you were probably going to be fine.

Still, there was worry there. It made her both anxious and somehow very tired; it had been a long day at work, capped off with the phone call from the police. Honestly, she just wanted the day to be over. She checked the clock on the living room wall and saw that it was 10:20—a little earlier than she preferred to go to sleep, but she figured with a melatonin in her, she could get to sleep and wake up in the morning with the good news that the killer had been caught. She could then resume her daily life, a life of work and an endless stream of worry about paying for doctor's visits, worrying about only her liver and whether or not she'd get a transplant before her liver caused an extensive hospital stay in about three or four months.

Jesus, maybe a killer might solve a bunch of these problems.

It was a terrible thought, but she was unable to keep it from coming. She'd noticed a bent towards darker humor in the days following the last test—the test that told her the outlook wasn't going to be great unless she could get a liver transplant.

"I'm going to head to bed," she told Ryan, leaning over and kissing him on the cheek.

"You want me to come with you or stay down here to keep an eye on things?"

"That's what the cops are for."

"Yeah, I know, but…"

He trailed off here, looking to the window she'd been peeking out of and then back to her. She knew he wanted to be the biggest help he could be. It was probably not enough for him to know there were cops out there. Cops were not something he could control. But the Smith and Wesson tucked in the cushion about four feet away from him was totally within his control.

"You do what you want," she said. "But I think we're okay."

"Maybe I'll just finish watching the show and then come on up. You okay?"

"Yes, I think I am."

She found just how true this was as she left the living room and started upstairs. Again, she felt like someone walking close by a hornet's nest, keeping their distance and feeling that they were going to be safe, despite the constant buzzing. She walked into the bathroom and brushed her teeth, working her way through her nightly routine. She passed through the upstairs hallway the same way she had, on autopilot, as she'd been going through the same process for twenty-one years now.

It was because of her familiarity with the process that she knew something was off the moment she stepped into her room. She reached for the light switch by the doorway, but something stopped her hand Not only did it *stop* her hand, but it captured her and pulled her forward.

As she went stumbling forward into the darkness, her arm still held tightly, she saw the shape. A head, shoulders, an arm racing forward.

Christina opened her mouth to scream for Ryan but the sound of it was interrupted by the sudden appearance of a blade passing through her neck. It did not slice her—she was only faintly aware of that during the final three seconds of her life; it had been shoved into her neck, passing all the way through. The sound of it was deafening in her ears as the life passed out of her, right along with the warm blood that seemed to erupt from her neck as the dark shape in front of her faded into the rest of the rushing darkness that suddenly appeared as if from everywhere, swallowing her up as she fell to the floor.

CHAPTER SIXTEEN

Rachel was sitting in the front row of a funeral—of her own funeral. Everyone was wearing black and there were a few people softly weeping. Paige was sitting beside her, and Peter served as their daughter's other bookend. A preacher stood in front of them behind an ancient-looking podium. Rachel's casket sat between the pastor and the gathered crowd, and everything was deathly quiet. She heard something very similar to scratching coming from inside the casket, but it was soon drowned out by Paige.

She was speaking to Peter, looking up to him with tear-soaked eyes. "Daddy, she should have told us sooner."

"I know. But she was a very selfish woman, sweetie. Let this be a lesson to you. Keeping secrets is toxic. It'll kill you in the end."

"Why didn't she tell us?" Paige asked.

Peter only shrugged. When he finally answered Paige, he turned directly to Rachel and looked her in the eyes. "Because she thought she was protecting you. But really, deep down, your mother was nothing but a coward."

She heard that scratching come from within the casket again. This time it was followed by her own, dry voice. It sounded distant and very far away. "Please…forgive me. I'm sorry…*so sorry…*"

Somewhere in the cemetery a bird began to chirp. It was insanely loud, the sound of an enraged hawk. Rachel stared at the casket and watched a small crack start to form down the side. She caught just a glimpse of herself inside, her body withered and her hair falling out.

The bird continued to wail and wail and—

It was her cellphone.

Rachel sprang out of sleep, clutching at her rampaging heart. For a sickening moment, she could still see the casket in her darkened hotel room. The final words of the dream echoed through her head in Peter's voice, making her dizzy as she straddled the line between dreaming and wakefulness.

"Your mother was nothing but a coward."

Her phone continued to ring, insisting she join the world of the waking. She reached out blindly for it and answered it without looking to the caller display. It was in the very last moment, as she brought it to her ear, that her still-trembling heart warned her that it could very well be Alex Lynch.

"This is Agent Gift."

"Agent Gift, it's Deputy Stanhope. Sorry for the late call, but we've got another body."

Was it late? She glanced to the bedside clock, the numbers blaring an angry shade of red that told her it was 12:02 at night. She'd only gotten two hours of sleep, but it had been more than enough to usher in the nightmare. In front of her, the TV was still on, which was rare for her. She usually hated any sort of noise when she was trying to sleep. God, had she simply drifted off again with no clear intention of sleeping? What was wrong with her?"

You mean aside from the cancerous tumor in your head?

She did not like that it was Jack's voice saying this in her mind.

"Is the victim on the list?" she asked, quickly coming awake. For a moment, she felt like she was plummeting downhill on a rollercoaster as her heart surged with fear and adrenaline.

"Yeah, Christina Ragland."

"Were there cops outside of her house?"

"Yes," Stanhope said, clearly perplexed. "And her husband was also in the house when it happened. But the killer was never seen and—"

"What's the address?" she interrupted.

Stanhope gave it to her and ended the call sounding as if he might slowly be losing his patience with the case. Rachel certainly understood the feeling. How could a woman be murdered in her own home when her husband was there with her and with cops parked outside the house? The mystery of it all woke her up even faster. She called Jack, placed it on speaker phone and spoke with him as she splashed water in her face and got dressed.

"I was sleeping," Jack said.

"So was I. But Stanhope called."

"We get a break?"

"Sort of. We have another body. Christina Ragland. And she's on the list."

"Give me five minutes."

He ended the call and almost right away, Rachel could hear him moving around on the other side of her bathroom wall, rushing to get dressed and head out.

Rachel moved quickly, allowing less than three minutes to pass between getting off of the phone with Stanhope and slipping her shoes on. As she got to her feet and hurried to the door, the world swayed a bit and her head felt suddenly heavy. She stumbled backwards just a few steps and sat down on the edge of the bed. It was an area of the room she was getting very familiar with.

The headache came quickly but was gentle. There was no dizziness, nor any white or black stars rocketing across her field of vision. It was just a disorienting feeling, as if her body was trying to tell her to hold the hell on a second.

To her, it was her tumor speaking up. *Remember me?* it seemed to be saying. *You can work like normal and pretend all is well, but I'm still here. Just wanted to remind you.*

She took a deep breath and lowered her head, waiting for the dizzy spell to pass. When she finally looked back up, everything seemed to be okay. There was a very minor headache lurking in the darker corners of her head, but that was about it.

There was a knock at the door just as she got to her feet. "Rachel?" Jack asked from the other side. "You about ready?"

She opened the door, relieved to find the dizziness gone and the threat of a headache slowly dissolving. "Yeah," she said. "Let's go."

***

The Ragland residence was fourteen miles away from the motel, but the lack of traffic so late at night made for a speedy trip. When they arrived, there were already four cars on the scene, including the one that had been parked right outside when Christina Ragland was murdered. Rachel was grateful for their presence because it allowed someone else to try to anchor the wailing, shocked husband while she and Jack ventured upstairs to where the body had been found.

She and Jack walked over to the patrol car parked on the side of the street—presumably the one that had been there while the murder had occurred. Rachel showed her badge as she approached them. The driver rolled his window down, a look of suppressed guilt on his face.

"You guys saw nothing?" she asked.

"Not a thing." The guy behind the wheel was middle-aged and clearly didn't like the accusatory question. Maybe it was because he also looked a little spooked and confused. "Our eyes have been on that damned house since nightfall and we saw absolutely nothing."

"He's right," the cop in the passenger seat said. "A stray cat crossed the western tip of the lawn around nine thirty. That was the most action we saw all night."

Rachel nodded and headed across the lawn, to the concrete sidewalk. Jack followed behind, taking his time to look around, giving the yard a casual scan. When they entered, there were two cops in the downstairs den with a man she assumed to be the husband, His head was buried in his hands, and he was making a sound that was a mixture of a wail and a hissing intake of breath.

One of the cops saw them, nodded, and pointed to the stairway at the right edge of the living room, where the room joined the kitchen. At the top of the stairs, she and Jack simply followed the murmur of soft voices to the bedroom at the end of the hall.

Stanhope was already there, standing with another uniformed man in the Ragland's master bedroom. The second man was older, easily close to sixty, and was looking down to the body with a grim sadness. A gray moustache dropped low as he frowned, and it remained there when he turned to greet Rachel and Jack.

"Agents Gift and Rivers, this is Captain Brown," Stanhope said.

"Good to meet you," Brown said without much emotion. "If either of you can figure out how the hell this happened, I'd be much appreciative."

Rachel stepped further into the bedroom and got her first glimpse of the body. Christina Ragland appeared to be in her forties, with blonde hair and brown eyes. The brown eyes were wide and staring up at the ceiling. There was a streak of still-wet blood in her right eyebrow. There was also a great deal of blood on the underside of her chin, having splashed there from the wound in her neck. It was a clean cut but even without proper cleaning or a closer look, Rachel could tell that the stab wound was a vertical cut rather than a horizontal slash.

The light blue carpet was soaked in blood on all sides, pools and splatters of it leading to the edge of the bed. The window on the right side of the bed was opened, allowing a cool breeze to meander into the room.

"Has anyone gotten anything of note from the husband yet?" Jack asked.

"A bit," Stanhope said. "He said his wife came upstairs somewhere between ten and ten thirty. He stayed downstairs until a bit after eleven. Watched a show on TV, set up the coffee for the next day, and came upstairs. He says he went to the bathroom to get ready for bed and guesstimates the time he went to bed as being just a bit after 11:30. He made it two steps into the room before he saw her."

"And he heard no signs of an intruder?" Rachel asked.

"He says he didn't," Stanhope said.

"And I personally spoke with the two men that were stationed outside the house," Captain Brown said. "Had some stern words with them, but they both swear up and down that they saw no one enter the house. And to be honest with you, I do believe them."

"When did they arrive at the house?" Rachel asked.

"Around 6:30."

Rachel walked over to the opened window and looked out of it. She guessed the drop down to the yard waiting below was about fifteen feet or so. No more than twenty. It was a drop that someone could easily survive, but likely not without a break or sprain or some other injury to their legs. However, over to the right, there was the slanted roof of a screened-in porch that covered almost the entire back side of the house. That, in addition to the thin strip of roof between the screened-in porch and the bedroom—which was really little more than a decorative way to run the gutters along the back—would have made it easy to get from the window down to the ground in a much more manageable way. Getting from there up to the window was a totally different story, though. Especially when there were cops parked outside.

She looked at the window and window-frame, but could see no clear signs of forced entry or remnants of fingerprints or dirt of any kind. She then poked her head out of the window and looked to the edges of the frame. It was hard to tell, but she thought she saw some scratching and just the slightest bit of indentation along the base.

"Any security cameras around here?" she asked.

"They have a Ring doorbell on the front door," Stanhope answered. "We had an officer just finish up looking over all of the footage right before the two of you arrived, and there's nothing on it. The last motion it detected was when the husband got home."

As Jack started making a circuit of the room, Rachel pulled out her phone and looked at the transplant list. Christina Ragland was the fourth name on the list. She'd noticed this before, back at the motel, but it seemed somehow much more important now that they were standing in the woman's bedroom with her dead body at their feet.

"I'm going to get down there and have a look at the back yard," Jack said.

Rachel only nodded at him, slowly looking around the room. It was a sizeable bedroom, with a large walk-in closet. There was no bathroom, but she'd seen the master bath when she'd come up the stairs and down the hallway; it was the second door on the right just before the bedroom. She looked in the walk-in closet and saw nothing noticeably out of place. The wife's clothes were on the right, the husband's on the left. It was all separated by a few pieces of luggage and a small rack of shoes.

The same was true of the bed and the area around the window. Other than the fact the window was open, there seemed to be nothing strange or out of place. From what she could tell, nothing had been stolen, though this would of course have to be confirmed by the husband. But based on the initial state of the bedroom, Rachel felt certain the sole purpose of the killer coming here was to kill—not to rob the family.

She thought of a man standing in this bedroom, knife in hand, waiting. If the cops had not seen him arrive, chances were good he'd been here a while. And if he'd escaped through the window, chances were also good that he already knew the layout of the back yard and the screened-in porch. The entire scenario screamed of a killer than knew the house, meaning the killer either knew the family very well or had scouted out the location a few times before acting. She looked over to the large closet and wondered if the killer had perched in there, waiting for the right moment. But if that were the case, he would have been in there for a very long time based on the series of events the husband had laid out.

"When did the police come into the house?" Rachel asked, again looking to Christina's body.

"Well, the husband knew they were out there," Stanhope said. "The way all three of them tell it—the cops and Ryan Ragland himself—Ragland went running out of the house, screaming for them to come inside. They say he made it about halfway down the sidewalk before he apparently changed his mind and ran back inside. They say when they got into the house, he was running back up the stairs to be with her."

"Both of them came in?"

"Yes."

"I went down that same path of thought," Brown said. "It's regrettable, as the ideal situation would have been for one of them to stay out there in the event the killer was trying to escape. But like I said…they've had a stern talking-to."

Rachel nodded, looking back to the window. "What if the killer remained inside until he knew the cops were coming into the house? What if he escaped through the window mere seconds before the cops came in?"

"I just want to know how long he'd been waiting," Stanhope said. "He doesn't show on the doorbell camera and according to Mr. Ragland, that window was never opened throughout the day."

"I assume he'll say it was closed when he discovered his wife's body?"

"One of the men parked outside the house asked him that," Brown said. "Mr. Ragland says he feels certain it was closed, but he was so distraught over what he'd found that he can't be sure."

"When I head downstairs, I want to check windows on the first floor. The layout of the back of the house makes it harder to get to this window but it would be pretty easy to quickly get out of it."

Rachel took one last look at the body. The single neck wound appeared to be the only attack. And though she was no forensics expert, she was quite sure the flow of blood from the body indicated that the knife had gone all the way through the neck, from front to back.

"How far away is forensics?" she asked.

"Last I heard, about five minutes," Stanhope said.

"I'm heading out to join Rivers. When they get here, let me know if they find anything. If the killer was in this house, waiting for God only knows how long, he had to have left *some* trace of himself."

"Absolutely."

"And another thing to consider," Rachel said, the idea coming just as she headed for the bedroom door. "This woman was higher up on the list. Number four, in fact. It makes me think we need to put the first three on the list under protective custody."

"It's a good idea," Brown said, "and we can certainly try. But as I'm sure you know, the person we want to put under protective custody has to agree to it. We can't *make* them."

"Yes, I know. We'll just have to convince them of how serious it is."

What she thought but did not dare say as she looked down to Christina Ragland's body was: *And I don't think that should be so hard.*

CHAPTER SEVENTEEN

Rachel headed back downstairs to where Mr. Ragland was still being consoled by a cop. Rachel heard only a fragment of the conversation and ascertained that Mr. Ragland's mother was on the way over to be with him. Meanwhile, Rachel walked into the den area and looked at the window. She opened it and checked both sides of it, but could see nothing out of the ordinary. She did the same with the single hallway window but there was nothing there, either.

She hit what may have been paydirt when she checked the kitchen. There were two windows there—one looking out over the side yard and another, smaller one, over the sink. The one looking out onto the side yard was about eight feet off the ground and hard to open. Still, she saw nothing that raised suspicions.

However, when she checked the one over the sink, things were a little different. There was nothing on the interior, but she noted a few scratch marks on the outside, just at the corner. She closed the window and stepped outside onto the screened-in porch to get a better look. Sure enough, there were light scratches that looked rather fresh There was also a very slight chipped section, right at the edge of the frame where it settled into the windowsill.

She walked to the wooden door that connected the screen porch to a small, uncovered section of porch but saw nothing out of the ordinary there as well. It made her wonder if the Ragland's didn't lock the screened-in porch or, if the scratches on the window *were* evidence of the killer breaking in, how he might have got to the window in the first place.

When she got out to the back yard, she saw that Jack had made the assumption she'd made. When she stepped down from the screened-in porch, she saw him looking up to the thin stretch of shingled roof that ran as a connector between the second-floor windows and the roof of the porch. He looked over to her as she came across the lawn, which was lit up by the back porch light. She noted at once that there were no security lights or flood lights. She wondered if the killer had known this and if it's why he'd been able to leave with such confidence through the bedroom window.

"He already knew the layout of the house," Jack said. "More notably, *the back* of the house."

"Yeah, I figured that, too. I think he somehow got in through the kitchen window and then escaped with this route," she said, nodding to the section of roof they were observing. "But it sort of makes sense. With the first two victims, our killer somehow knew about doctor's appointments. So he's doing his research before he attacks. These aren't just random acts of passion."

"Well, of course not. I mean, he had to get his hands on that transplant list. The very fact that he has a list suggests there's been a lot of planning in this. He also would have had to know about Webber's and Ramirez's appointments."

Looking up to the roof from the vantage point of the yard, another thought came to Rachel. "You know, if we take another look at the list and the killer is indeed on it, I think we'd be okay narrowing it down to someone in good shape and healthy enough to scale that roof."

"That's a good point. And based on the fact that there are now three people from the transplant list that are dead, I'm willing to bet our killer *is* on it."

It made every possible bit of sense, but something about it just didn't seem to sit right with Rachel. She couldn't quite put her finger on what it was, but it poked at some unrealized bit of logic, teasing the edges of her mind.

As they continued to look around the yard for any sort of clues— maybe a partial shoeprint or something mistakenly left behind by the killer—Rachel heard the screen door to the porch open up behind her. She saw one of the officers standing there, looking out to them. "Sorry to bother you," he said, "but Mr. Ragland wants to speak with you."

They moved to the stairs at once, Rachel taking the lead. "Is he speaking clearly?" she asked.

"For now. He finally calmed down enough to speak more than two sentences without losing his mind. When he heard there were FBI agents here, he asked to speak with you."

The officer led them back inside, through a large kitchen and then into a living room. Mr. Ragland sat on the couch, with two cops standing around in different parts of the living room. As Rachel and Jack entered the room, Stanhope and Brown made their way down the stairs. They all nodded to one another as they made their way out back as Rachel and Jack moved into the living room.

Ryan Ragland looked to be about the same age as his now-deceased wife, likely forty-five or so. His eyes were swollen from crying and he looked pale. As he regarded Rachel and Jack, Rachel notcd that one of the cops that had been in the room moved toward the stairs. She assumed he was the one in charge of making sure a heartbroken and distressed Ryan Ragland didn't try to bolt upstairs to see his wife one last time.

"Mr. Ragland, I'm Special Agent Rachel Gift, and this is my partner, Agent Rivers. You wanted to speak with us?"

"Well, sure. I need to know for certain whoever did this is going to be caught. It's not just that he took Christina from me tonight…but according to the call we got earlier, this makes three people, right?"

"That's right," Rachel answered. "So any information you could give us would be an enormous help."

"I already told the cops…I have no idea how this happened. No clue at all. We got the call and Christina saw the police car the moment it pulled up across the street. We had dinner, watched some TV, and then she went to bed."

"What time was that?" Jack asked.

"About quarter after ten. It was a little earlier than she usually turns in, but I figured the stress of the call from the police had something to do with it."

"And when she went upstairs, you stayed downstairs?" Rachel asked.

"Yes, for another hour or so. I think the call bothered me more than her. I don't know if she took it seriously or if it was just too unreal, or…"

He trailed off here, looking to the far wall, to the TV's blank screen. For a moment, Rachel was worried they'd already lost him. She could sense an immense wave of grief behind his eyes, but he managed to push it away for now.

"Mr. Ragland, I need to ask you a few difficult questions," Rachel said. "I understand if you can't get through all of them but—"

He waved her warnings away with a flip of his hand. "It's okay. Just go ahead."

"I'm wondering if Christina knew anyone else on the transplant list. Or did she even happen to know someone with a similar ailment?"

"No," he said, giving a very shaky smile. "Christina had something of a morbid sense of humor. She often joked about how hard it was to find support groups for women with liver cancer. As for any other people she may have met or spoken with at the hospital or at doctor visits, I couldn't tell you. If there *were* people like that, she never mentioned them to me."

"Can you think of any friends or family members that may have had something against her? Even if it might seem like a small thing to you."

Ryan opened his mouth to answer but then gave Rachel a curious, almost offended look. "No. I mean…what the hell sort of question is that?"

"Given the nature of the scene, we believe there is a very good chance the killer had been in the house for a very long time. Also, the way in which he escaped out of your bedroom window so quickly and without apparent injury makes it appear as if they knew the layout of your house very well."

"Oh, well I don't think…wait. You mean to tell me the killer could have been in here all afternoon?"

"Possibly."

"But how?"

"We don't know," Rachel said. "I'm curious, though. Do you usually lock the door on the screened-in porch?"

"Ah, that damned thing. Sometimes…when we think about it. But there's nothing out there worth stealing, really. So we usually just settled on the back door. But yeah…when one of us thinks about it after going out back, we'll lock it. It was…it was unlocked, wasn't it?"

"Yes, it seems that way," Rachel said. "You see, because there was no footage of anyone on your Ring doorbell, we assume he broke in from somewhere else. Maybe through the kitchen window off of the screened-in porch, or even the bedroom window. But as of right now, the only sign of breaking and entering we have that is remotely solid is the fact that the bedroom window was open when the police got upstairs. They say you *think* it was closed when you found her?"

"I'm almost certain of it…but I really wasn't paying attention to that sort of thing…you know?"

His face scrunched up and his eyes narrowed. Rachel knew they were going to lose him soon, and rightfully so.

"Oh my God…," he muttered. "I can't…I mean she…"

"You heard absolutely nothing out of the ordinary while you were down here by yourself?" Jack asked.

"No. Nothing," he nearly snapped. "I was watching television, but I had the volume down very low. I mean...," he let out a sob here and seemed to force out the rest. "I even heard her when she flushed the toilet and spit into the sink when she was brushing her teeth. I couldn't be—"

That did it. The mere mention of his wife brushing her teeth, of doing something so monotonous and normal, broke Ryan Ragland all over again. He let out a single, stifled cry before letting the next one out unhindered. He buried his head in his hands and screamed. When he got up to head for the stairs, Rachel saw that she'd guessed correctly. The officer by the stairs blocked him from going up.

Rachel and Jack shared a strained glance as Rachel let the hard facts of the moment settle in. Someone had killed a woman in her own bedroom and then escaped without being seen. In and out, despite the presence of a police cruiser parked across the street. And from what they could tell so far, the bastard hadn't left a single clue behind. In other words, it felt like a dead end despite the sudden burst of activity. And as the night crept beyond midnight, that dead end felt a little more resolute—like slamming a head into a brick wall.

Rachel nodded her head towards the door, and Jack walked over to meet her there. "Any ideas?" he asked.

"Just one," she said. "I think we need to go back to the coroner."

***

It took a few phone calls and some very grumpy replies from the other end, but Rachel managed to touch base with the graveyard shift coroner on duty. She and Jack left the Ragland residence had headed back to the coroner's office at 1:45 in the morning. The on-duty coroner seemed both irritated and elated that he had company—two conflicting emotions all at once that somehow seemed to fit the personality needed for someone to work such a job in the late-night hours.

"I regret to inform you," he said as they entered the larger observation room, "that the body of Bruce Webber has been moved to the funeral home. His services are scheduled for the day after tomorrow. I get the impression that the family just wants to move on and give him a proper burial."

Rachel had not been expecting this, but it didn't matter in the grand scheme of things. As long as they had digital photos of the wounds prior to clean-up, they should be okay.

As for Maria Ramirez's, the coroner had already taken the liberty of bringing the body out. Rachel looked to the wounds, which had been fully closed and dressed. Two in all, the same as when she'd viewed them before.

"The one to her stomach…was a very deep one?" she asked.

"Not too deep. Deep enough to do damage, but when compared to the cut at her neck, the one along the stomach seemed almost accidental."

Rachel nodded to the laptop sitting on the small rolling desk. "Can you bring up Webber's pictures?"

"Sure. Before or after?"

"Both."

He did as he was asked, sipping from a small mug of coffee as he did so. "Is there anything in particular you're looking for?"

Jack sidled up next to her and whispered into her ear: "I was about to ask the same question."

"I'm not quite sure yet. If I'm recalling it all correctly, it seemed to me that Bruce Webber was pretty much butchered. How many wounds in all?"

"Six. Four of which could have been deadly. And the one to the neck was gruesome."

"In other words, he got a much worse treatment that Mrs. Ramirez. And when we compare that to the new body of Christina Ragland, the method of murder gets even cleaner…simpler. Just one wound—albeit a brutal one—to the neck."

The coroner turned the desk towards them, showing the pictures from Webber's body. There were many of them, and they showed the workings of a man possessed. In comparison, the body of Maria Ramirez looked almost untouched. Christina Ragland had been even cleaner.

"It seems like he's getting more control over himself when he kills," she said. "I think with a progression being shown now on three bodies, we can rule out the notion that maybe he just held something against Webber that he didn't against Ramirez."

"So he's getting better?" Jack asked.

She eyed the closed-up wound on Ramirez's neck. It looked tight and precise. And if the one along her stomach had been accidental, it meant that the killer had wanted to go for the neck from the start.

"This cut was rather clean, right?" she asked, nodding to the woman's neck.

"Yeah, it was," the coroner said. He clicked around a bit and brought up two images side by side: one was Ramirez's neck wound directly after the murder and the other was the closed-up, clean one. Even the grisly picture made the wound look almost delicate.

"Any suggestion what sort of knife might have been used?" Rachel asked.

"No. But this one to the neck damn near makes you think it might be a scalpel, huh?"

"Yeah, it does," she said, glad that he was confirming her new suspicion in a roundabout way. Because even if it wasn't a scalpel—and the wound to the stomach indicated that it probably wasn't—it did point to one clear thing.

This killer knew what was doing. Whether it was scoping out the schedules and homes of his victims or the precise way in which he seemed to be developing in going straight for the necks, it made Rachel come to a conclusion that might be a stretch but, in the moment, felt right.

Yes, he knew what he was doing. Maybe a little too well.

"I know that look," Jack said. "What is it?"

"I think we need to look at the transplant list from a different angle," she said. And then, after some thought, she added: "And maybe the names of people on the list that are in the hospital aren't as safe as we thought."

CHAPTER EIGHTEEN

As they left the coroner's office and drove back to the police station, it became abundantly clear that this was just going to be one of those cases that wasn't going to allow them to sleep. Rachel was fine with it, as she was getting used to it. But she was already resenting the fact that when she did get back home, the first thing she'd likely do would be to sleep—not spend time with Paige or to figure out of there was any hope of reconciliation with Peter.

"So you know," Jack said as she drove back to the station. "Three of the people on this list have already been confirmed to currently residing in a hospital right now."

"Yes, but I'm not as interested in that as I am to know if any of them have ever had training or background in the medical field. Hell, maybe even to see if any of their immediate loved ones might fit the bill."

"It's a good theory, but that's a hell of a lot of cross-referencing."

"You got anything better to do tonight?"

"No, not really."

They arrived at the precinct and returned to the cubicle space Stanhope had given them earlier in the day. She was pleased to see that everything was still connected to the internal network, giving them access to the criminal databases. There were also numerous scribbled notes from throughout the day—some in her own handwriting, and some in the scribblings of some of the Roanoke PD officers. She was sure it probably all looked like one big mess to anyone unfamiliar with the case, but it was surprisingly tidy and put-together.

"Here's some food for thought," Jack said as they started digging in. "If our killer is indeed affiliated with a hospital in some way, why wouldn't he just start with the people on this list that are already there in the hospitals? Seems like it would be a hell of a lot easier than climbing a roof and sneaking in through bedroom windows."

"I agree with that," she conceded. "But the more I think about this, the more it makes sense. Think about it: the killer knew when the first two victims had appointments. That sort of information is going to be hard to come by unless you're a doctor or very closely affiliated with the places where the appointments had been set."

"Maybe," Jack said, but he did not sound very convinced.

As Rachel continued to dig through records and fighting through notes on the people on the list that had been jotted down earlier, it became painfully clear that it was going to be hard to get any sort of confirmations without speaking to the people or their families. In other words, they'd need to all be called again. And though she was dedicated to the case and would do just about anything to close it, she was not about to call these poor people at 3:10 in the morning.

As she found herself blocked time after time by a lack of information, she feared that she was just going to have to eat three or four hours. It wouldn't be so bad, she supposed. She could go back to the hotel and get some more sleep and call the people-of-interest right away.

"Hey, Rachel, did you see any of this earlier today?" Jack asked.

She looked up from her notes and saw that he was thumbing through a file folder. A small sticky note was affixed to the front of it. Someone had written *For Dep. Stanhope* on the front of it.

"What is it?" she asked.

"Not sure. It's looks like a list of random cases at first. Bullet-points and names, things like that. But it was with Stanhope's notes from our cross-referencing today. I'm guessing he had someone dig up recent cases that may have involved sick people. Maybe he just got it late. Let's see…"

He set the file down and typed a case number into the database. The three pages of reports that popped up told them a sad story of someone that had been arrested for attempting to steal insulin from a pharmacy back in 2019. The man had not been armed, had gone to court, and paid a three-thousand dollar fine. The man was diabetic and could not afford the outrageous prices for his insulin so, having had enough, decided to try bullying a pharmacist for it. The tale was told in brief sentences, bullet points, and just a few lines of testimony from a pharmacist.

"Jesus," Rachel said. "How many of those are there?"

"Not many. Seven in all. But I'm guessing whoever made the list had a reason for compiling them."

That said, he continued inserting case numbers into the database. As he did this, Rachel looked over the small list. None of them went back more than three years. Two of them indicated that the person responsible for the crime was currently in prison. "I think it's safe to skip these," Rachel said pointing to those two cases.

"Yeah, okay," Jack said distantly. "Hey, I need you to Google a name for me."

"What's the name?"

"Joseph Quinn. He's a surgeon that apparently assaulted the family member of a patient. I've got the report here and it…it really doesn't make much sense."

She typed the name into the Google app on her phone, adding *Roanoke, VA,* into the search terms. She got over one hundred hits and though the headlines of the first few gave a pretty good snapshot of why he'd been listed in a police database, she read the first article she came to. She read it out loud and the deeper she got into the article, the straighter she sat up.

"All charges were dropped against Dr. Joseph Quinn this week, as he and the family of Rita Stone reached a private settlement. Five months ago, following what Dr. Quinn himself referred to as a 'massively botched surgery,' Rita Stone died on Dr. Quinn's operating table. According to Albert Stone, the husband, Quinn was borderline antagonistic when he delivered the news to the family. This resulted in a verbal argument and then an assault in which Dr. Quinn threw three punches, one of which dislocated Mr. Stone's jaw. It was later discovered that Dr. Quinn had been working on very little sleep and taking caffeine pills and supplements to stay awake, as he was dealing with the recent loss of his wife, who had passed away rather suddenly from a diagnosis of Crigler-Najjar Syndrome—a potentially fatal disease of the liver. Later reports indicated that Dr. Quinn had his medical license revoked and that it could have been part of the agreed upon settlement.

"As the situation unfolded in the months following the assault, it also came to light that Dr. Quinn had been seeing a psychiatrist. Quinn later revealed that he'd needed to take an entire month off of work after his wife's passing, trying to get back into the right mental state to perform surgeries. 'It was tormenting me,' Quinn stated, 'that we'd made calls to get her on a transplant list, but she died before her name was even placed on it.'"

Rachel looked away from the article. There was another paragraph, but she doubted anything it had to say was going to hit as hard as the last comment she'd read. Jack, wide eyed and clearly feeling as if they were on the brink of a breakthrough, looked back to the police record in front of him.

"This is a report of the assault. Quinn stated that he, and I quote, *sort of blacked out for a moment when speaking with the Stone family. The husband got in my face, understandably angry, and I just snapped.*"

"He knew loss, too," Rachel said. As an agent, it was never a good thing to feel one certain way about a potential suspect, but she felt incredibly sad for Joseph Quinn in that moment.

As she thought on this for a moment, she allowed herself a moment to rest. She'd become something of an expert at catching quick cat naps and somehow waking herself up with some sort of internal alarm. She dozed lightly for a moment, her mind never too far away from the case. She found herself thinking of Joseph Quinn's story and found herself nearly sympathizing with him. To lose someone so suddenly, there was no sense in trying to move on with life as usual.

Funny you can't figure that out about your own family, she thought. *How are they going to pick up and continue after you're dead just because you're stubborn and won't look into treatment options?*

These sharp internal thoughts yanked her out of the little bit of rest she'd managed to find. Even as she got to her feet, knowing they were going to have to pay Quinn a visit, she checked her watch and saw that it had somehow come to be 5:50 in the morning. Sure, it was too early to go visit Quinn but then again, if the report and the article were spot-on, Dr. Joseph Quinn was someone she had no issue waking up so early in the morning. Sob story or not, his history made him a prime suspect in the case.

As she started leaving the cubicle in search of Jack, her phone rang from inside her pocket. When she saw on the caller display that it was Director Anderson calling, she answered it right away. She knew that adding her Alex Lynch drama on top of everything else was a huge mistake, but she also knew she needed answers. Even if she could just file one of her questions about the Lynch situation away as *solved*, it would be a small relief.

"This is Agent Gift."

"Gift, it's Anderson. I know it's early, but I have a message saying you need to speak with me about the Alex Lynch situation."

"Yes, sir I do. I don't know what the hell is going on at that prison, but he managed to call me again. Even after he somehow got someone to put that squirrel and note in my daughter's room, he managed to call me."

The heavy silence on the other line told her all she needed to know; this was obviously news to Anderson as well, and he was furious. "What did he say?"

"He was just teasing me. Telling me that if I threatened him in any way, he'd send a big man to my daughter's room to assault her. And you know, I'd love to think it was nothing more than an empty threat, but after that squirrel…"

She also couldn't help but think of a killer striking in the Ragland house while there were cops parked right along the side of the street.

"I'll look into it," he said, and she could hear the fury in his voice. "You have my word on that. If I have my way on this, heads will roll."

"Thank you. And you'll keep me updated?"

"Yes. And while I have you on here, I should tell you that we do have a very small break in that Alex Lynch case. There were no fingerprints found at the scene but ironically enough, we did find two hairs on the squirrel. They both belonged to the same man—a man with quite a track record by the name of Edward Walton. I currently have a search out for him as we speak. He lives somewhere in southern Virginia, pretty close to the Carolina border. And again, I'll keep you posted on that as well."

"Thank you, sir."

"You need to come in, Gift? This is pretty heavy stuff."

"No, sir. I'm fine. Just keep me posted on everything you can as soon as you get updates, please."

"Of course."

They ended the call and Rachel had to reorient herself to what she'd been doing before the call. Jack noted this bit of confusion and stepped in close to her. "You good?"

"Yes," she said trying not to snap at him. She was glad he cared, but she was just about done being seen as this poor, fragile little thing. "And I'll be a lot better once we get to have a word with Joseph Quinn."

With that, she started down the hallway again, pocketing her phone and doing everything she could to keep her mind focused on the case. And with Joseph Quinn serving as the next stop, she couldn't help but hold out a little bit of hope.

CHAPTER NINETEEN

Joseph Quinn's house was not at all what Rachel had been expecting. It was a small two-story townhome in a middle-class part of the city. As she drove into the parking lot, she even wondered if they'd gotten the wrong address from the precinct's records. Stereotypical or not, Rachel had been expecting a large house somewhere near the hospital, as was the case with most surgeons. She'd figured that even if he'd been suspended and no longer worked in medicine, he'd likely still own his house. Then again, who knew what sort of money was exchanged behind closed doors in terms of settlements back when Quinn had gotten into his trouble.

It was 7:52 when they knocked on his front door. As they waited for an answer, the small rectangular parking lot in front of the row of townhomes was quietly busy with people leaving for work and beginning their morning routines. A few of them looked towards Rachel and Jack as they stood on Quinn's stoop, waiting. It would make for great gossip later in the day, Rachel supposed.

When Quinn hadn't answered after thirty seconds, Jack knocked again. Rachel looked down to the parking lot and saw that it appeared that each townhouse had two parking spaces for each unit, positioned right in front of each home. Several cars were gone likely already having left for work. But she noticed that the two in front of Quinn's town house were empty She'd noted it on the way to the door but had thought nothing of it at the time.

"Looks like he's already left for the day," she commented.

"Looks like it. But I wonder…what does a disgraced surgeon do for work? It's got to be hard to do anything other than surgery, right?"

"I'd think so. Maybe we can find out where he works and have a word with him there."

Jack shrugged, giving the door a defeated look. As they turned to head back to their car, the door to the neighboring townhouse opened up. A thirty-something woman came out with a computer bag over one shoulder, her free arm used to hold the hand of the little girl that followed her out of the door. The girl looked to be no older than five and carried a small lunchbox in her right hand.

"Excuse me, ma'am?" Rachel said.

The woman looked over to them and a look of interest instantly came across her face. She looked to the parking lot, then to Quinn's front door, and finally back to Rachel. "Hi," she said. "Can I help you?"

"Hopefully. Would you happen to know your neighbor, Mr. Quinn?"

The woman rolled her eyes, still gripping her daughter's hand. "Not like a friend, no. But I know him enough to not be surprised that there are very official-looking people on his doorstep on a weekday, looking for him. What are you, FBI or something?"

"Yes, or something," Rachel said, showing her badge.

"And why are you not surprised to see us here, exactly?" Jack asked.

"Well, he tends to come in very late and isn't very quiet about it. There have been two times in the last month or so when he's come home drunk out of his mind and screaming at his door because he can't get the key in. And a few months back I came out to leave for work and he was passed out in his car with puke all down the side of the driver's side door."

"How long have you lived next door to him?" Rachel asked.

"Not too long. He just moved in about eight months ago."

"And did you ever speak to him *before* you had these complaints about him?"

"Just once or twice. He seemed like a nice enough man at first. And you know, he might be. He just seems to have a really bad drinking problem."

"Did he ever say anything to you about what he used to do for a living? Maybe some trouble he'd been in?"

"Not really. One of the times I came out to shush him for screaming at his door, he said something about how if he just had an operating table, he'd be able to figure it out. I figured it was just some drunken rambling, you know?"

Rachel was about to ask a question when the little girl started pulling at her mother's arm. "C'mon, let's go!"

"One second," the mother said. And then, to Rachel and Jack, "Sorry. She loves her pre-school teacher. And actually, I'm running a little late if I want to get to work on time. So I sort of need to go."

"One more question, if you don't mind," Rachel said. "When you confronted him about his late-night noise, was he ever hostile towards you?"

94

"Oh, no, not at all. If anything, he was understanding and apologetic. It's one of the reasons I've never filed a complaint or anything." She frowned and gave a sad little shrug. "I think he has a problem, you know?"

"I don't suppose you happen to know his bar of choice, do you?" Jack asked.

"I do, actually. It's another thing he randomly mentioned during his ramblings. He said he's putting the kids of the guys that owns Spillman's through college with his bar tab."

"Spillman's," Rachel said. "That's a local bar?"

"It is. Is Mr. Quinn…I mean, is he okay? He in some sort of trouble?"

Neither Rachel nor Jack responded. Rachel only nodded and gave the little girl a smile. "Thanks for your time," she said.

They headed back for the car and sat there for a while. Rachel sipped at the powerful coffee she'd taken from the station and tried to think of next steps. It might be easy enough to figure out where Quinn was working these days, but that was going to be wasted time. And she was becoming all too aware of the fact that time was a very precious commodity.

"I think we call Stanhope," he said. "See if we can figure out where Quinn might be working now. In the meantime, I think a visit to this Spillman's place is smart. Maybe get a feel for where and how he's been spending his time."

"I know you're not much of a drinker, Rachel, but most bars aren't really open at eight in the morning."

"But don't some open for lunch? Maybe we'll get lucky and find someone working there that's prepping for lunch.'

"I say it's doubtful, but I agree that it's better than sitting at the station and leafing through files and reports, hoping to find something of use."

"So you pull up the directions to Spillman's, and I'll call Stanhope."

Jack nodded without much enthusiasm. Even Rachel understood it wasn't much of a plan, as neither option was likely to offer any real results. But to be so early in the morning, it did feel encouraging to have some sort of strategy in place, no matter how desperate it seemed.

***

95

Spillman's was conveniently located just two and a half miles away from Quinn's address. It was a very subtle sort of building, the kind you might miss unless you were specifically looking for it. It was a small building located between an old barbershop that looked to have been closed down, and an empty lot with a For Lease sign on the corner. Even as she parked in front of it, Rachel could tell it wasn't open. Still, they'd come out here so she figured they may as well knock on the door to see if the owner or proprietor was inside.

She knocked on the door as Jack peered through the plate glass along the right side of the building. Waiting for an answer at the door, she saw a small waiting area directly in front of the glass and then a surprisingly large bar area. There were a few tables set up off to the right, positioned in a way that made it clear this place was a bar first and restaurant second—the sort of place that probably offered subs, burgers, and fried stuff just to keep their clientele satisfied.

There was no one moving around inside following her knock. She was pretty sure no one was inside—unless they were in the back in a storage room or cooler or something.

"Hold on a second," she said. "Let me see if there's a back employee entrance."

"Sure. And if you get in, grab me a drink, would you?"

She smirked at him as she made her way to the empty lot on the right side of Spillman's. Almost right away she could see that there was indeed a small parking lot behind the bar. When she came to the back of the property, she saw that the parking lot spilled over behind the closed-down barber shop as well. There were two vehicles there—an older model pickup, and an older-model BMW.

There was a single door located directly in the center of the bar's back wall. A tattered metal sign attached to it read Employees Only. She even saw a small buzzer installed along the frame presumably for delivery drivers. She pressed the little buzzer and knocked hard on the door. She waited a few seconds and then knocked again. But by the time the echo of the knocking faded, she was sure there was no one inside.

She turned to head back to the front but paused when her eyes passed by the BMW behind her. The passenger side was facing her, but she saw something on the ground from under the car on the driver's side. She ducked down a bit to look under the car and took a slight step back.

It was hard to tell for sure without getting a better look, but she thought there was a body on the ground on the other side of the BMW.

She made her way around the car quickly and sure enough, there was a body sitting on the ground, propped up against the side of the car. She thought it was dead at first, but then saw the heavy rise and fall of the chest. It was a man, his head tilted hard to the right. He looked to be middle aged, with five-o-clock shadow scruff on his face.

Rachel hunkered down in front of the man, wondering if it might be a late-night drinker that hadn't trusted himself to make it home but was too proud to call a cab.

"Hey," Rachel said. "Excuse me, sir. Wake up."

He didn't respond at first, but when Rachel reached out and nudged his shoulder, his head lobbed over to the other side. His eyes fluttered open for a moment and when he saw Rachel, he backed harder against the car. His eyes grew wide as he took in his surroundings.

"Sir, are you…?"

He didn't exactly strike out at her, but he made a pushing gesture that nearly connected. It was so unexpected that Rachel stepped back, but it wasn't enough space to miss the reek of alcohol coming off of him as he let out a shout of surprise. By just the way he stumbled and then broke into a run as if his limbs were made of rubber, Rachel could tell the man was disoriented—probably still drunk from the night before. And as this realization settled in, she thought of what Joseph Quinn's neighbor had said about him stumbling home at ungodly hours and shouting at his door. She knew it wasn't a guarantee that the man currently starting to run away from her was Joseph Quinn, but she thought the chances might be pretty good. There had been pictures of Quinn with the articles, but those pictures had been of a professional and well-kempt man. The man ambling away from her was clearly drunk and disheveled.

Rachel sprang up to her feet and chased after the man that might be Quinn. He wasn't very fast, ambling across the parking lot with drunken speed and cutting in the direction of the empty lot. When Rachel started running after him, she was more irritated than anything else. Chasing after a drunk man this early in the morning…sometimes the life of an FBI agent really could be borderline comical.

She caught up to him as he was about halfway through the vacant lot. Jack had caught on to what was happening and came rushing toward them as well. Rachel grabbed the man by his shoulder and spun him around. She intended to pull her badge and let him know that running from the FBI was not a smart move. Instead, the man fell to his knees, made a retching sound, and threw up. He narrowly avoided getting it on Rachel's shoes. She leaped back, finding herself uncharacteristically angry and having to restrain herself from kicking out at him.

Jack apparently found the puking slightly offensive. He stepped between them with a sour look on his face, maybe sensing Rachel's desire to kick him. "What's your name, sir?" Jack asked.

The man spit out the remnants of vomit form his mouth and wiped his lips on his forearm. He chuckled nervously as he looked around the lot. Rachel could see understanding and clarity slowly come swimming into his eyes. "Shit," he said. "Not the best way to meet someone, is it?"

"Your name, sir," Jack said.

The man winced and looked up at them like an embarrassed child. "Joseph Quinn," he said. And then, sighing, he said, "You guys cops or something?"

Rachel took one wide step around the puddle of vomit and reached for her handcuffs. "Something like that. Mr. Quinn, we have some questions for you. I'd really like for you to come with us easily. I'd feel bad cuffing a man in your condition."

"Yeah, I'd feel bad, too." He eyed them again, scanning them as if trying to determine the level of trouble he might be in. "What's this about anyway?"

"Just come with us, sir."

Quinn looked back to the back lot of the bar and sighed again. He got to his feet and took a moment to reorient himself. "Let's go. You won't get any problems from me."

Jack placed a hand on Quinn's shoulder and led him forward. Rachel followed, hoping such an odd start to the day might serve as an omen of sorts and bring them some good luck.

CHAPTER TWENTY

Rachel had been waiting for the moment Quinn would throw up again, this time in the back of their car. Fortunately, he managed to make the ride without making a mess. He asked several times why they needed to speak with him but neither Rachel nor Jack answered. And honestly Quinn didn't seem to mind the lack of answers right now. Rachel assumed that heading to a police station couldn't be any worse than sleeping by the side of his car in the back lot of a bar.

He got out of the car without any objection and only spoke up again after they walked through the front doors of the station. The smell of coffee filled the hallway on the way to the interrogation room and he responded right away.

"Any chance I could get some coffee? And water? And maybe some aspirin?"

Rachel and Jack shared a look, trying to decide without speaking who would try to get these things. Usually, neither of them catered to the whims of someone they were about to question, but it was clear that Quinn was in bad shape. Jack gave in pretty easily, not because he thought Rachel would argue him on it but because Jack had, ever since they'd started working together, made sure not to toss out any "go fetch" tasks or anything that seemed like housework on her.

"Fine," he said, cutting his eyes at her as he veered off to the break room. Meanwhile, Rachel found a set of three interrogation rooms near the back of the building, a corridor adjacent to a row of holding cells.

Rachel noticed that Quinn looked perplexed when they stepped into the room. From her experience, men that had seen such a room at least once or twice before seemed to enter them with an almost resigned sense of acceptance. But when someone was hauled into an interrogation room for the first time, there was a sense of dread to them. Their posture was usually very straight, and their eyes tended to wander, as if looking for an escape route. She saw same of this in Joseph Quinn. He did not sit down behind the table in the center of the room right away. He simple stood by it, looking down to it as if he didn't trust it or the chair behind it.

"Have a seat, please, Mr. Quinn."

He did as she asked, sitting slowly in the seat. He grimaced a bit when he was settled, presumably fighting off a roaring hangover.

"Okay," he said. "Now that I'm here, will you tell me what this is about? Am I in some sort of trouble because I slept behind the bar? I mean, I couldn't get into my car because—"

"Hold on, Mr. Quinn. Let's save that for when Agent Rivers returns."

He looked genuinely worried for the first time. Rachel wondered if some of the haze of his condition was starting to wear off now that he was a bit more awake and aware of his situation. At the same time, the confusion on his face was genuine, too. The hangover and lingering drunkenness were making it hard to get a read on him but for the time being, Rachel was starting to think he may honestly have no idea why he was here.

Jack came into the room less than a minute later. He held a Styrofoam cup of coffee in one hand and a bottled water in the other. He set them both down in front of Quinn and then reached into his pocket where he took a small packet of individually wrapped Tylenol. "This is all they had in the pain reliever department," he said.

"Thanks," Quinn said, somewhere between embarrassed and grateful. He took the meds first, tearing the packet open and popping the two pills into his mouth. He sipped cautiously at the water with the experience of a man that had chugged too much water after a crazy night out one too many times.

He then pulled the coffee over slowly but seemed hesitant to drink it just yet. Rachel took a seat in the chair on their side of the table. With only one chair on each side, Jack was left standing.

"Okay, Mr. Quinn," Rachel said. "Before Agent River came in, you were about to tell me why you'd been sleeping outside of your car. Can you finish that up for me?"

"The bartender saw how bad off I was and called me a cab. When I refused to take the cab, he got my keys." He frowned here, searching. "I'm still now sure how. I remember him kicking me out, telling me he called another cab, and it was up to me to catch it. But I didn't. And I don't...Jesus, I don't even remember seeing it. And when I realized I still didn't have my keys after he closed up shop, I got the bottle of whiskey out of my trunk, had a few nips, and just sat down for a while." He looked to both of them, clearly embarrassed now, and added: "And the next thing I know, you were waking me up."

"Does this sort of thing happen often?" Rachel asked.

"Not to that level, no. I mean, the bartender has taken my keys before, but I always get them back at the end of the night just before I get into a cab."

Jack stepped forward and Rachel could tell he was taking great efforts not to come off as sounding judgmental. "You used to be a surgeon, right?"

"That's right." There was no pride in his voice of expression, just sadness. It was almost as if the memory of the man he'd once been pained him to even think about.

Jack nodded and said, "We know your story and everything that happened. But we're not here to go over all of that. We're here because we need to ask you about a series of murders that have taken place over the last few nights."

"Murders?" he asked. He spoke the word as if it sounded strange to him, maybe a foreign language. And as the reality of why they'd brought him here slowly sank in, a slow and creeping fear started to spread across his face.

"We are quite certain people are being killed because of their placement on a transplant list for a liver," Rachel explained.

"Oh my God. You know this for sure?"

"Yes," Rachel said. "And we also know that one of the reasons for your fall from grace was the loss of your wife—who passed away from Crigler-Najjar Syndrome. We can—"

"Please don't presume anything about my wife."

"Did she not pass away because of her liver?"

"She did," Quinn said, showing more coherence that he had all morning. "And we failed to get her on the transplant list on time." He took a moment, cringing again, and shook his head. "Are you assholes suggesting I'm killing people now? Just because I lost my temper at a patient's family?"

"We're suggesting nothing right now, Mr. Quinn," Jack said. "But you were a doctor once, so I assume you're a fan of logic. In our search for answers, we discovered that it appears the victims are being selected because they are all on a transplant list. The three victims were all dealing with liver-related medical issues. At least one of them has been treated at the hospital you once worked for. During your troubles, you made it no secret that your wife was—"

"Okay, yes, I get it. It makes sense that you'd ask me. But it doesn't help me to like it."

"Why did you run when you saw me there in front of you this morning?" Rachel asked.

"Honestly? Because you scared the shit out of me. I woke up with my head roaring and my stomach all jacked up from the night before. You woke me up and all of a sudden there's someone in my face. I freaked out and just ran. I'm certainly not proud of it, but...well, as I'm sure you can guess, there are many things about my recent past that I'm not very proud of."

"Can you give us proof of your whereabouts for the last three or four nights?"

He chuckled and reacted, his head in his hands, one hand on either side of his head as if he were about to massage his temples. "Sadly, yes. Well...except for three nights ago. I was at home but there isn't much proof."

"What about the evenings, like around four or five?" Rachel asked.

"Yeah. Just about any day of the week, I'm either at Spillman's, the Outback Steakhouse up the road, or another bar called Tully's Place. I start around five in the afternoon with dinner and most nights it lasts until at least nine or ten." He chuckled again, but it sounded like he might be on the verge of tears as he had to vocally admit how he spent his free time. "And sadly, I've been present and accounted for at every single one of those places this week."

"What about around four thirty or five three days ago?" Rachel asked, thinking of Bruce Webber. She figured that timeframe was more likely to trip him up. "Where were you?"

"Three days ago? I was at Spillman's. Happy hour specials include highballs."

"Anyone that could back that up?"

"For sure. I can give you the bartender's name and the names of at least three others."

"How about the few nights between then and last night?" Jack asked.

"Yeah, like I said...all except the night I was just hanging out at home."

Rachel watched Quinn's face and could see the shame plastered across it. More than that, though, she could see a slight tremor in his hands. It could just be nerves from being interrogated by the FBI, but she thought it was most likely part of his alcoholism. And if his condition was so bad that it was causing him the shakes, there was no way he could have killed the last two victims—not with the sort of precision the killer had displayed.

Throw in witnesses to his time at the bars over the last few nights and one thing became clear: Joseph Quinn was not the killer. They still did not have a killer in custody, and they were quickly running out of time.

That thought struck a note in her head and made her pause for a moment. Every other thought in her head fell away for a moment as she focused on it. *Quickly running out of time...*

What if that was exactly what their killer was dealing with? What if their killer was acting out in such a frantic schedule (three victims in just four days) because he was running out of time? Or, if they were killing in the hopes of assisting someone else, what if the person they were killing *for* was running out of time? "Mr. Quinn, sit tight for a second, would you?" she said.

Quinn nodded, finally finding the courage to start sipping at his coffee. Even in that simple little motion, she could still see the slight trembling of his hands.

Rachel left the room, noticing Jack's confused expression as he followed her out. She closed the door and took a few steps away from the interrogation room before she turned back to Jack.

"Yeah, I didn't think it was him, either," Jack said. "Anyone that quick to say he has several people to back up his excessive time at the bars that *isn't* telling a lie isn't going to look that ashamed of himself."

"That and the shakes. Did you notice them?"

Jack shook his head and frowned. "What's with the look? You got something new?"

"Maybe. I want to have another look at the transplant list. I think we might be sorting out the names wrong."

"How's that?"

"Maybe we don't try analyzing them over who is a victim and who the killer might be. What if our killer is working so quickly because he or a loved one is running out of time?"

It took Jack a few seconds to catch on, but a gradual look of encouragement crept across his face. "So we need to find out who on that list is the sickest."

"Exactly," Rachel said. "We need to see if we can find out who on the transplant list doesn't have much time left."

CHAPTER TWENTY ONE

"Don't take this the wrong way," Stanhope said, "but you two are FBI. I mean, you know how impossible it's going to be to get that sort of information about people currently on a transplant list, right?"

Rachel nodded but would not be sidelined so easily. She'd been working with the bureau long enough to know that getting medical records for the living were often much harder than acquiring medical records for the recently deceased. She'd worked cases where it had taken her upwards of five days to get medical records to help with a case. And she did not have that sort of time to waste on this one.

They were sitting around the cubicle space that had essentially become the hub of operations for the case. As they tried to talk things out, Rachel noticed yet another thing she liked about Stanhope; it was clear that he hated sitting around and talking. He was the type of officer that wanted to be out on the streets, trying to do *something* no matter how much of a waste of time it seemed to be. She identified with it and respected it.

"We'd need another warrant, for starters," Jack said, sounding slightly chagrinned. "And something like this is going to probably require the approval of a judge."

"That wouldn't be an issue for us," Stanhope said. "The judge that would be in charge of it is a huge supporter of the local police. But still…another warrant means another two days *at least.*"

"And we don't have that sort of time," Rachel said.

"And on that note," Stanhope said, "let me go ahead and give you a bit more bad news."

"Ah Jesus, *more?*" Jack asked.

"Yeah. We've got eight people on the list that have refused the police protection and custody. They feel like it's an overreaction. There were two that seemed downright scared when we told them what was going on but didn't want to deal with the added hassle of a police presence while they're also dealing with health issues."

Rachel looked to the printed list in front of her—specifically to the names that had been crossed out. "Do you think they'd be okay with an additional visit…maybe from the FBI this time?"

"Can't know for sure. Why? What are you thinking?"

"I'm thinking that even though it would feel like a colossal waste of time, we need to speak to everyone remaining on this list. We need to figure out who might be in the worst shape. I know that sounds awful, but—"

"No, I agree," Jack said. "It might be a waste of the rest of our day, but it would be faster than getting the warrant cleared."

"I can get a few officers on that to help," Stanhope said. "To this point, all but a few of our contacts with them have been over the phone. We can get in on some of the face-to-faces, too."

It was a daunting task to even think about, made worse by the fact that Rachel knew she would be away from home for at least another day. The sting of it was too much to push away and before she could let it overcome her, she got to her feet. "Excuse me for a moment, would you?"

She stepped away from the little cluster of cubicles and found a quiet place in the hallway. When she pulled out her phone, the mere idea of calling Peter to give him an update made her feel incredibly anxious, but she made herself pull the number up and place the call. Her heart seemed to drop a bit with every ring in her ear as she waited for him to pick up. And when his recorded voice asked her to leave a message, she was a bit too relieved. She opted not to leave a message; it was the easy way out, and Peter would not hesitate to tell her so. Making sure not to let it slip her mind, she set an alarm on her phone to try calling Paige's sitter at six that afternoon—because Lord only knew where she'd be by that time of the day.

Yet as she pocketed her phone and returned to Jack and Stanhope, she wondered if Peter had truly been unable to come to the phone or if he was avoiding her calls. At first, it didn't seem like such a terrible thing. But then she wondered how long he would do it. She wondered if Peter, in his hurt, would do something stupid like take Paige somewhere else and just never reach out to her, or never return her calls.

It was a terrifying feeling and she found herself trying to blame it on the actions of Alex Lynch. She didn't doubt that if Lynch had not come into the picture, Peter may not have made the rash decision he'd made. Yes, he may still be upset that she'd waited so long to tell him about the tumor and he would be upset about her decision not to get treatment for it, but he may have stayed. She felt that her involvement with Alex Lynch and the subsequent danger to their family is what had truly set him off.

Of course, it did no good to think of such things right now. She walked back to the cubicles, already overhearing Jack and Stanhope doling out names for each of them to visit. Before she rejoined, she took a moment to gather her own thoughts and feelings on the matter The whole concept of *running out of time* was a bit too close to her, after all. She wasn't sure she liked picking and choosing based on who may have the least amount of time because it ran the risk of overlooking other factors. But in this situation, she thought it was definitely the safest. It was yet another example of her own fears and secrets getting in the way of her judgement—another reason she needed to come clean and tell Jack, Paige, and probably even Director Anderson about her diagnosis.

But not now. Now, there was this case. Now, there was trying to figure out how to handle her family in the midst of her situation.

She heard Peter in her head, sad and cold at the same time. *Not now?* his voice scoffed. *If not now, then when? Don't make your daughter wait until you're dead to find out the secret you were keeping.*

It was a thought that chilled her. And even when she rejoined Jack and looked to the transplant list again, she still felt it. Looking at it, she wondered if that's what she was slowly becoming as she tried to bury her situation with work: just another name on a list, waiting to die.

CHAPTER TWENTY TWO

The voice had become insistent last night, so loud and prominent that he'd not slept well. One question seemed to run through his head over and over in a desperate sort of whine: *Why are you making me wait so long?*

There were a few times during the night when the voice had been so clear that he'd gotten out of bed to see if she was in his bedroom. But there had only been the darkness, divided up by the thin blades of light coming through his partially closed blinds. When seven o' clock had come around, he knew there was no way he'd be able to function at work. He called in sick, bemoaning a headache and stomach pains.

He'd then had a few cups of coffee and a bowl of cereal, consuming it all at his kitchen table. While he ate, he thought of the Ragland woman. More than that he thought of how he'd narrowly avoided the police. He'd heard them coming up the stairs just as he'd dropped down to the slanted roof over the screened-in porch. Another ten seconds, and he would have been caught. Ah, but that was the excitement in it, wasn't it? Hell, he'd even driven by the house afterwards, her blood still on his hands, and watched the cops come in and out of the house.

He knew what he wanted to do today, and his success at the Ragland house made it easier to really get a grip on it. He knew exactly what he had to do, and what it was going to take to get the voice to calm down. And while it was indeed becoming easier, that did not mean he particularly enjoyed doing it. But the voice did not understand that, and even if it did understand, it would not give a damn.

The voice did not care just how much work he'd put into killing the Ragland woman. And that was a damned shame, because he considered it a feat in and of itself. He'd played the scene over and over in his head, from the start of it all to the moment he rolled by the house in the dark, cop lights flashing, his hands bloody.

He'd been unable to find any appointments within the next few weeks, so he'd settled for breaking into her home. Because he'd staked her house out several times in the past week or so, he knew when her husband got home. That meant he had to break in early. He'd parked his car in a small subdivision half a mile away, walked to the house, and made sure to stick to the side of the yard in order to avoid the Ring doorbell. Breaking in hadn't been very hard either because he'd been able to let himself in through the kitchen window with his little screwdriver. He'd nearly fallen into the kitchen sink as he crawled in over the counter, and then made his way upstairs where he'd waited in that damned closet for about six hours.

But the voice did not care about that sort of thing. It would never be pleased, and he could never do enough for it.

He dressed for the day as the tension of what he had to do built within him. The nerves he felt were no different than the nerves that came with a sudden doctor's or dentist's appointment. Ah, but underneath it...wasn't there just a tiny bit of excitement? He knew there was, but he did not want to admit it to himself.

He drove twenty-five minutes, to the outskirts of the city. It was a rundown neighborhood with what he'd always thought of a saltbox-houses—one-story deals with one or two windows along the front and thin, shingled roofs. He supposed the non-PC crowd would refer to it as the "poor part" of town. Truth be told, he'd only ever come through here in order to locate the woman on the list. He'd come by a few times just to familiarize himself with the lay of the land. He knew it was a dangerous neighborhood and that he'd need to be careful. So what better time to strike than now, this early in the morning. He figured any responsible people in the neighborhood would already be out and about on their way to work and the troublemakers would likely still be asleep.

She lived on a little back street, bordered by the back yards of houses positioned in front of the street, and a heavily weeded lot and a chain link fence along the back. Further behind it all, a paper mill churned like a gray smudge against the morning, giving the neighborhood a smell that was part mildew and part exhaust. He could smell it even through his closed windows.

He took a left onto her street, drove a few houses down, and nearly slammed on the brakes.

The last thing he'd been expecting to see was a police car parked in front of the house. He briefly wondered if the old woman had kicked the bucket—if she'd saved him the work and gone out on her own. But he also knew that if that were the case, there'd likely be an ambulance on the scene as well.

Of course, maybe the cops had just been the first on the scene. There were just too many questions to ignore. So, rather than coming to a stop in the middle of the road, he drove further down the street. He pulled into an empty driveway, backed out, and parked on the same side of the street the police car was on. There were only seven spaces between them—three of which were empty—giving him a clear view of the house.

Coward.

It was the voice, poking and prodding. While he would much prefer the woman had died of her own accord, the voice found any idle sitting and patience a sign of weakness. The voice wanted immediate action, he understood it, but he also knew he had to think logically if he wanted to appease it—to appease *her.*

He did his best to ignore her nagging persistence as he sat in his car and watched the house. After a few moments, a single policeman stepped out. He was a tall African American man, fairly young. He turned to say one last thing to whoever stood on the other side of the door—either the ailing woman or her husband, he supposed—and then made his way down to the patrol car. This excited him because he figured it meant the officer would be leaving. But after thirty seconds, the car was still there. It still remained a minute later, and then three minutes after that.

When the police car was still sitting there ten minutes after the policeman had come out of the house, he had a very bad feeling as to what was happening. It seemed the woman was being placed under police protection.

He gripped the steering wheel tightly and kept a shout of frustration from rising up out of his throat. Sure, he'd expected some police interference at some point, but not this soon. If this woman was being protected, what about the others? Were there truly enough expendable police officers to send out to protect everyone he had in his sights— everyone the voice insisted needed to be done away with?

He glared at the police car, as if willing it to burst into flames. This was going to make things so much harder, and she was going to be so disappointed in him. She'd be mad as hell, too, but the disappointment was what he feared the most.

You screwed around and waited too long and now look what happened, she said as he stared at the car. He could just see the shape of the cop inside as he tried to figure out how he could adjust his plans.

He could still get it done, but he was going to have to take some very drastic measures.

But as long as it made her happy, he was willing to try just about anything.

CHAPTER TWENTY THREE

Rachel sat behind the wheel of their parked car, once again studying the transplant list. It was starting to feel more like a puzzle of some kind than a list. She had a new print-out and was starting over with her selection process. But before she committed by marks to the page, she looked over to Jack and shook her head.

"Don't take this the wrong way," he said, "but you look like you're looking for the answer to a crossword clue right now."

"I was just thinking that's exactly how I feel."

He looked out of the passenger side window, to the lush and well-tended lawn beside them. The sixty-one-year-old man inside was fine with a police presence sitting outside of his house, so long as they didn't knock on his door and want to ask him questions all of the time. They'd spoken to him and the daughter that was caring for him and now they were just waiting for Stanhope to send a patrol car over to relieve them. It was yet another positive about Stanhope: he understood that the FBI were their guests and, as such, should not have their time wasted by surveillance tasks when there were cops available to do it.

"So here's what I'm thinking," Rachel said, tapping her ballpoint pen against the list. "I think we can cross off anyone who is actively under protective custody. As of right now, that knocks eleven people off the list right away—as potential victims, anyway. I still say we need to consider the fact that if the killer *is* killing for someone else, the person they are killing for might not even know."

"Good point. Also, according to Stanhope's last update, it could be as many as thirteen people within the hour. He and Brown don't have many men to work with, but the ones they do have are busting their collective asses."

"Right. Now, I initially thought we could also cross off people that were currently in the hospital, but that isn't necessarily a safe bet."

"Seems safe to me," Jack said. "Why isn't it again?"

"It still seems like someone would need to have some sort of connection to a medical organization of some kind in order to be able to get the transplant list. Not only that, but it seems to me it would be a bit easier to take out people if you had them trapped in a hospital room."

"I agree with all of that. But it conveniently ignores that none of the victims have been killed in a hospital."

"No…but two of them were found *outside* of medical facilities."

"Good point."

"And that's why I'm not fully prepared to take those people off of the list just yet."

She crossed out each name that had agreed to police protection and then circled the names of the victims. She read over each victim and tried to think of some way they might be linked. Also, she found it odd and refreshing that while in Jack's presence, she could look over the list and not be assaulted by the sorts of thoughts that had stormed through her head the previous night—thoughts of chemo and sickness, of trying to make a go of beating her cancer so Paige might have a chance at having a mother and a somewhat normal childhood.

Bruce Webber, a sixty-three-year-old man. Maria Ramirez, a thirty-three-year-old woman. Christina Ragland, a forty-one-year-old woman. At first glance, none of them had much in common (aside from the bum liver). The age range was spread around fairly well, only excluding the very young and the elderly. None of them were especially wealthy, and from what the records showed, they had a few different doctors, though Ailsworth did show up on a few of them.

"Hey, Jack, do you remember the age of the youngest person on the transplant list?"

"Um…" he said, looking through his own thin stack of papers he'd brought with him from the precinct. "That would be Michael Reeding. Nineteen years old and suffering from a genetic disorder. Right slap-dab in the middle of the list. Why?"

"And the oldest?"

He frowned at her ignoring his question, but looked back to the sheet he currently held. "That would be a Mrs. Pam Jones. Eighty-three. And she's number eleven on the list. Why?"

"Just trying to see if there's anything similar to the people he's gone after already—or the people he's maybe skipped over. Based on what we have so far—which isn't much, I admit—it looks like he's fine with taking out middle-aged women and older men."

Jack thought it over, looking back to his paper and adding: "That doesn't really tell us much, though."

"No, not yet. I mean, we have no one younger than thirty and that's not saying much, true. But we—"

The ringing of her phone interrupted her. She'd spoken with Stanhope so many times in the past two days that she recognized his number this time. She answered it quickly, hoping to knock another name off of her list.

"Hello, Deputy Stanhope."

"Hey there, Gift. Thought you'd want to know that I just got off the line with Captain Brown. He just got word that a gentleman by the name of Antoine Evans got the call this morning. They found a matching donor for him and he's currently in surgery to receive it."

Rachel looked to her list and saw that Antoine Evans was second on the list. So, positions one and two were now off the list, along with the three victims and those under police protection.

"Also," Stanhope said, "we've got two more on the list that can be added to the protection list." He gave the names and Rachel marked them off, realizing that she was now looking at a very short list indeed. If she took the gamble and assumed it was not anyone currently in the hospital, then it became a very manageable list.

In fact, that would leave only five people on the list—two of which were listed below Christina Ragland. She eyed the five names carefully. As she studied them, she was fully aware that not only were they potential victims, but one of them could very well be the killer.

"Gift? You still there?" Stanhope asked in her ear.

"Yeah, sorry. But with those two names protected and Mr. Evans getting the surgery, that only leaves us with fives names."

"Yes, but Mr. Wan and Mrs. Breedlove denied our services…so…"

"Any chance they're worth looking into?"

"Well, Mr. Wan is pushing eighty, so I doubt he's the killer. And Mrs. Breedlove is sort of a bitch, among many other things, but she can barely breathe with the state she's in."

Rachel considered it all for a moment and put boxes around their names on the list, which left her with only three. If it came down to it, they could go back and check the family and loved ones of Wan and Breedlove. But for now, she had a gut feeling that it was these final three that needed to be looked into. She also speculated that if Mrs. Breedlove was indeed in terrible shape that maybe the killer was associated with her. This harkened back to an earlier theory she had considered: that the killer may be knocking people off of the list in order to help someone else—someone that might be in very bad shape.

"Does Breedlove have any children?" she asked.

"A daughter that lives in New York."

"Husband?"

"No. I believe he passed away two or three years ago."

She filed all of this away as she looked to the remnants of the list. She considered one of the names heavily: Seth Dillinger. It was a name that stood out because his was one of the few names that had come back with a red flag due to a criminal history. He'd had a sex offense charge eight years ago. It was the only ding on his record but now as his name stood out among just two others, she couldn't help but wonder if there was something there.

"We've got Wilson, Dillinger, and Smith," she said. "If Agent Rivers and I take one of them, can you take one and send someone else to get the last?"

"I'm sorry, but no. Not right now, anyway. I mean, with the surveillance on all these people, I'm out of manpower."

Jack shrugged and hitched a thumb at himself. Rachel nodded and said, "On my way out to my listing, we'll swing by the station and Agent Rivers and I will split up. Can you call ahead and make sure he has an accessible car?"

"Will do. Talk to you later. And your backup is en route. I'd say given them another five minutes or so."

She ended the call and started the car. "You think you can handle speaking with someone without me just this once?" she joked.

"Are you kidding? I'll probably do much better than I would *with* you. Without your dry, get-down-to business-demeanor, I think my boyish charm tends to come through more."

She wasn't able to keep the genuine laughter from coming out. Jack put on a mock expression of hurt, clutching his heart.

"You wound me, Gift."

She bit the laughter back, realizing it was the first genuine laughter she'd allowed herself over the past four or five days. And while it felt incredible, she also knew that such moments were going to be few and far between in the coming months. So she let it sink in and joked back and forth with Jack in that small window of time as they waited for another policeman to show up as their relief.

CHAPTER TWENTY FOUR

Rachel watched Jack rush through the front doors to get a precinct car to go check in on his assigned person from the trio off of the transplant list—an older man by the name of Percy Wilson. She pulled away from the curb and started speeding to the address she'd selected—the address of Seth Dillinger.

According to his record, he'd been arrested and charged for sexual misconduct eight years ago. He'd met a woman at a bar, gave her a ride home and they'd messed around in his car. When she failed to invite him inside to keep things going, he did not take no for an answer at first. He did not rape the woman, but only because she was able to fight away from him and unlock the power doors in his pickup truck. She'd fallen out to the street with a bruise on her wrists and hips from the skirmish in his truck.

That was all Rachel knew about the incident and, quite frankly, it seemed pretty cut and dry. She'd seen nothing about jail time served and assumed Dillinger was like a surprising number of men in that position—so scared over the repercussions he'd faced that he did everything to avoid such a moment again. Of course, she also had to rely on the knowledge that most murderers did tend to have at least some form of criminal activity in their past, often small and seemingly insignificant.

She thought all of this through as she made her way to Dillinger's address, a small subdivision that looked as if it were one step away from being little more than a trailer park. It was the sort of dainty neighborhood that tried a bit too hard to look much more refined than it actually was. The lawns were mostly green and well-kept but most of the houses told a different story.

Rachel came to Seth Dillinger's address and parked. When she stepped outside, she found the street quiet, aside from a barking dog somewhere in the distance. A small Ford pickup truck sat in the driveway, parked in front of a small, closed garage. She peered in through the passenger side window and saw nothing out of the ordinary: an empty soda bottle, a phone charger cord, a balled-up burger wrapper on the floorboard. It was the sort of old truck that made it hard to tell if it was used all of the time or hardly ever used and was severely neglected.

Moving on from the truck, she walked to the front door and knocked. She got no response, but the presence of the truck in the driveway told her there was very likely someone home. She knocked again and this time even tried the door. It was locked, but there was a rattle along the inside of the door. She thought this might mean the interior of the lock had been damaged at some point in the past, and if she wanted, she could probably pick it rather easily. If she was more confident that Dillinger could be the killer, she might have gone to such lengths.

As she waited again, she continued to hear the dog barking. It seemed to be closer this time. When she looked down the street, she saw a woman walking a dog. It was a bulldog, trundling along in front of its owner. Rachel knocked again and this time called out as well.

"Hello? Mr. Dillinger?"

Roughly two minutes had passed since her first knock. Maybe he wasn't home after all. Maybe he owned a second vehicle and was at work. She reached for her phone in her pocket to call in the update and ask if someone could figure out where Dillinger worked. As she came down the porch steps and to the sidewalk, though, the woman walking her dog stopped just shy of Rachel's car.

"You looking for Seth?" the woman asked. She was pretty, and somewhere near middle-aged. She was wearing a pair of very tight joggers and a sporty tank-top and had the look of a woman that walked or ran several times a week.

"I am, actually. Do you know him?"

"Not well, thank goodness. Just enough so that he leers at me every now and then when I pass by. Gotta give him credit, though; he hasn't yelled out anything sexist or repulsive in a few years. Anyway…I can tell you for sure he's not home."

"You're certain? How?"

"An ambulance came by about an hour and a half ago." She hitched a thumb back behind her and said, "I watched it all from my porch. They wheeled him out and put him in the back."

"What?" Rachel asked. This seemed like a very big event in the case, even if she hadn't quite made up her mind about Dillinger. "You're sure?"

"Well, yeah! You can't really mistake an ambulance, now can you?"

"Did you happen to know that he was sick?"

"I'd heard, yeah. My neighbor is a really kind lady—Christian, donates to charities and missions, things like that. She'd been going by to drop things off for him a few times a month. Meals, stuff like that. I think it was something to do with his liver. Not sure. I know he was really bad off a few months back, but my neighbor said he was getting much better lately."

Rachel nodded, now hurrying for the driver's side of her car. "Thank you."

"Yeah, yeah. Is he dead or something? Who are you, anyway?"

Rachel didn't answer. She closed the door, started the engine and pulled away from the curb. She veered in the road a bit as she pulled out her phone and placed a call to Stanhope. The deputy answered on the second ring with the speed and tone of a man that was putting out a hundred fires at once. "Hey, Gift."

"Deputy Stanhope, I just visited the home of Seth Dillinger. He never answered the door but when I was about to leave, a woman on his street told me there had been an ambulance here less than two hours ago. She said she saw him rolled out of the house on a stretcher and into the ambulance. I need you to confirm it for me, please."

"That's news to me. Hold a second, would you. Let me get a confirmation on that."

"Sure. Any clue which hospital he would have been taken to?"

"Probably just Roanoke General. If you head that way, I'll let you know for sure in about one minute."

"Perfect."

There was a click as Stanhope ended the call. Rachel then immediately called Jack. She knew him well, so didn't expect him to answer until the fourth ring. Despite his devil-may-care attitude about most things, he was a tee-totaler when it came to obeying traffic laws. Sometimes he'd totally ignore incoming calls if he was driving, even if he was in the middle of a case. Right away, she could tell that he had her on speaker when she answered, so he wouldn't have to hold phone.

"Miss me?" he said in lieu of a greeting.

"You wish. Look...I got to Dillinger's place only to find that he was rushed to the hospital less than two hours ago."

"Jesus. Do you know what happened?"

"No clue. Stanhope is trying to figure all of that out for me as we speak. I'm very likely going to be headed to the hospital when you're done on your end. But keep me posted all the same, okay?"

"For sure. Same with you. Someone on the list...being sent to a hospital. I mean, it *could* be a coincidence, but..."

"Yeah, I know." Her phone beeped in her ear as Stanhope was already calling back. "Stanhope is beeping in. I'll talk to you later."

"You using hands free?" he asked with a smile in his voice.

"Of course not." She ended the call and switched over to Stanhope as she came to the exit of the subdivision. Things suddenly felt as if they were moving far too fast, that the end was hurtling towards her at the speed of light. "Deputy?"

"Okay, here's all I know. Seth Dillinger called for an ambulance at 8:45 this morning. He complained of feeling faint and a sharp pain coming from his liver. From what I was just told, he was on the mend from toxic hepatitis but apparently took a turn for the worse. He was in stable condition when he arrived at the hospital but that's the only update I have. Apparently, the doctors are still looking him over as we speak. And I was right; he'll be at Roanoke General."

"Got it. Thanks, Deputy."

She ended the call and pulled up directions to the hospital. She didn't quite understand the sense of urgency she was feeling, but trusted her gut on it. She thought that Dillinger being rushed to the hospital might rule him out as the killer, but she also couldn't help but bring up one of her original theories—that the killer may be linked to a hospital or medical facility in some way. And if that was the case, she'd imagine that one of the easiest times to strike would be during check-in or immediately after being given a bed.

Running out of time…running out of time…

It had been a constant thread to this case, and she felt it heavier than ever as she sped toward the hospital. It reminded her of the case she'd taken immediately after discovering she had a tumor in her brain; she recalled how she'd felt something very much like a physical presence with her in the car, how it felt like the tumor itself was a person, always on her heels. She felt something similar to that now, like a pressure at her back as she felt her own mortality breathing down her neck just as heavily as the eventual outcome of this case.

CHAPTER TWENTY FIVE

Sometimes, it seemed that things just worked out for him. Even with her voice in his head, telling him how worthless he was, how much of a disappointment he'd turned out be, luck seemed to be smiling on him.

Less than twenty minutes after leaving the residence where the cops were parked out front, he'd parked discreetly in a fast-food parking lot, trying to figure out a new approach. He needed to act quickly because he feared if he didn't strike again soon, he'd lose his nerve. And if this entire ordeal came to an end, what the hell had all the planning and action been about? He would have killed three people for nothing. And she would never leave him alone. Her voice would haunt him and squash him until he lost his mind.

So he'd taken out his phone and opened up the very simple police band radio app. It just an app he'd downloaded on a whim two years ago. He hadn't been expecting much out of it but quickly discovered that when he adjusted the settings to a few specific locations and frequencies, it was a remarkable app. He'd spent some nights listening to police and ambulance chatter, even eavesdropping in on fire department frequencies. Listening in to the back and forth between ambulance drivers and police, he'd gotten the slightest taste of what he'd started working for ten years ago.

He'd gone to med school and found it much harder than he'd expected. Still, he'd done well, his sights on becoming a doctor so that he could help people. It was all the result of watching his mother suffer, of wanting to do something to help her—to ease the pain she'd been feeling for years as she'd battled a variety of illnesses and diseases. Nine years ago, she'd lost a kidney. A few years after that, diabetes had nearly taken her. And now there was her liver, actively poisoning her from the inside, slowed only by a variety of medicines that she could just barely afford. He'd helped as best he could, but the medicines and doctor's visits were wiping him out as well.

After a while, it had come to this…trying to do everything in his power to make sure she got a new liver. At her age and as weak as she was, he really wasn't even sure she'd survive the surgery, but it was the only chance she had.

He thought of her, alone in her bed right now, as he listened to the static-laced chatter on the police radio app. Over the years he'd listened to high-speed chases, a few shoot-outs, and multiple arrests. He'd also listened to the urgent conversations of drivers on the ambulance frequencies, rushing people to the hospital, arriving at the homes of those in need of assistance. If the course he'd chosen in life had gone the way it was supposed to, he would have been doing that. But his mother had gotten sick—*very* sick at one point—and he'd had to drop it all just to take care of her. He'd then picked up his meaningless job to just help pay for her bills.

He was listening to the app while sitting in the fast-food parking lot, hoping to hear some sort of banter about any sort of widespread police involvement in trying to check-in with certain people. He could not escape the nagging suspicion that they were on to him—that they knew he was using the transplant list to target his victims. And if they did know that and were actively protecting the people on the list…well, then, he was screwed.

And she would be *so* disappointed.

It took no more than thirty seconds before he did hear a few different snippets of conversation as officers talked back and forth to one another. Some were informing others that they'd arrived at specific addresses. At one point, his suspicion was verified when he heard one very specific exchange.

"Alright, I'm at the third address," a man with a very deep southern accent said.

"Which one is that?" came the reply.

"Ah…the seventh one on the list. Name of…"

"That's Myers."

"Yeah, that's the one."

The seventh one on the list…

So they did know what he was doing. It made him want to scream. All the work and time he'd put into this, and it was all going to go to waste. Panic, fear, and anger all waged war within him as he held the phone tightly and listened to the radio exchanges. And just before he truly gave into despair, there was another brief exchange that caught his interest—and gave him just a glimmer of hope.

"Hey, dispatch, this is Stanhope. I'm wondering if there's been any sort of chatter among EMTs in the last two hours about a man named Dillinger, Seth. Address is 1315 Castle Street."

"Checking on that now. Hold please."

As dispatch went away, another cop chimed in on the line. "Deputy Stanhope, this is Rogers. I heard that call earlier this morning. Don't know the details, but yeah. EMTs responding to a 10-52 on Castle Street. And I think the name lines up. You said Dillinger, right?"

"That's right."

Dispatch got back on the line, a female voice that sounded almost robotic on the line. "Deputy Stanhope, I have confirmation for you. Dillinger, Seth was removed from his home this morning and taken to the hospital. He called for the ambulance himself this morning. Seems he has a history with a liver issue. The ambulance carrying him arrived at the hospital fifteen minutes ago."

"Roger that."

That was all he needed to hear. He put his phone in the passenger seat but kept the app open and running just in case anything else of note was said. He pulled out of the parking lot, trying his very best not to speed. He was about fifteen minutes away from the hospital and knew the way well. He even knew where to park and which entrance to take.

He had, after all, volunteered there during med school. It had been several years since he'd volunteered in any capacity, but he assumed not much had changed. He ran the logistics through his head—where he needed to park, how he could manage to fit in without getting caught, how to pull it off and escape. It might take a few minutes of careful snooping and planning, but unless there had been drastic changes to the place, he thought it might be entirely possible to kill Seth Dillinger and get away. He knew that if he arrived at the hospital in dire need of that kidney, there was a good chance he'd be moved up the list. And how in God's good name was *that* fair to the others on the list?

Nerves sank in like stones in his stomach as he made his way to the hospital. He had the knife with him. He had, after all, been planning to use it elsewhere before he'd realized the police were on to him. But he doubted he'd use it. There was no way he could walk into a hospital with a knife on him. That was something else he was going to have figure out on the fly.

It's about time you manned up and got to work, her voice said in his head. *Of course, you waited too long and now the police are involved. Because of that, this will probably be the last one—so for God's sake make sure you do it right!*

He gritted his teeth against the tiring, grating sound of her voice. But he heard it all the same, her voice tearing him down and asking why he wasn't capable of more as he made his way to the hospital. He pulled into the main drive and bypassed the parking garage. He went around to the back lot on the eastern corner, where he'd parked multiple times when he'd been a volunteer. The only problem he was going to have was that he did not have the lanyard that volunteers were required to wear. But he thought he knew how to fix that when he stepped inside.

When he got out of his car, he walked to the rear entrance where most of the volunteers and some of the RNs would hurry out to leave for a quick lunch break when they didn't feel like heading down to the cafeteria. As he'd expected, there was no one there. He made his way inside easily and continued to walk with confidence, as if he belonged there just as much as anyone else. He was walking in this same manner when he walked into the second room on his right. It was a small changing room, not quite the size of the locker room the nurses used; that one was further down the hallway.

He'd changed in this room countless times and knew that spare scrub sets were kept in one of the little closets in the back corner. He walked over to it, hoping they'd changed nothing, and was relieved to find that it was all the same. He grabbed a set of scrubs, the cheaper kind that were pressed and sealed in a thin plastic bag and changed in one of the small dressing cubicles. It felt all too familiar, as if the years between his last time volunteering and now had passed by in the blink of an eye. He missed it more than he realized, the full feeling of that loss falling firmly into place as he stepped out of the cubicle in his scrubs.

As he left the room, he walked with his head down at an angle. He knew the number of volunteers in the hospital were limited. The chances that someone would see him and realize that he was a new face was fairly high. So he looked down, making his way to the elevators. He knew that anyone rushed in with a serious condition, hauled in an ambulance, would be taken to the second floor ICU at first—even if only for five minutes before they were moved elsewhere.

So that's exactly where he headed. All he needed was a weapon. And if he could keep his wits about him, he knew where to go for that as well.

Don't you overthink this, you idiot.

He truly hoped that when this was all over, the voice would stop. That hope was more than enough to help him push the nerves aside and to approach this coming murder with anticipation and excitement. By the time the elevators dinged as they reached the second floor, he realized that he hadn't been this anxious to kill ever since he'd started.

With a bit of a hurried spring in his step, he got off the elevator and headed in search of Seth Dillinger…and something to kill him with.

CHAPTER TWENTY SIX

Jack parked the basic sedan in front of the residence of Madeline Holcomb exactly seventeen minutes after leaving the station. Between the station and the Holcomb residence, he'd gotten the call from Rachel, updating him on the status of one of the other people from the list. Apparently, Seth Dillinger was on his way to the hospital—which, as far as Jack was concerned, pretty much ruled him out as their killer. But it also told him that they were really starting to weed the list down. One of two things were going to happen by the day's end: either they'd find the killer thanks to the list, or discover that the list may have absolutely nothing to do with the case at all. Though even Jack at his most discouraged and negative had to admit that it did seem as if the transplant list was the core to this entire case.

He stepped out of the car and looked at the house. It was a nice two-story, a mix-match of a few different styles. He thought it might be either modern beach house or some new-fangled approach to farmhouse. Whatever it might be, there were a few others nearby, the large lawns separated by perfectly trimmed hedges.

He knew very little about the woman he'd come to visit—just that her name was Madeline Holcomb, she was sixty-three years old and there was apparently something wrong with her liver—something wrong enough to have added her name to a transplant list, anyway. Jack imagined that if she did want the police presence outside of her home until the case was closed, he'd be the one to do it until a local was able to arrive. It was rather sad that he envied Rachel for having to visit the hospital for her guy while he was about to go and bother an old lady.

When he came to the door, he knocked loudly. There was no answer, so he then rang the bell. In doing so, it then occurred to him that an old woman living on her own and dealing with a liver-related illness may not be able to come to the door as quickly as most people. He reached out to ring the bell again but could just barely hear a ragged, female voice calling out from somewhere inside the house.

"My God, come inside already!"

Jack looked at the door for a moment, perplexed. If this was how she answered the door most of the time, surely she didn't have that many friends. Or maybe she had someone come by to check on her or help her out while she was sick and was expecting them. Whatever the case, Jack tried the knob and found the door unlocked. He pushed the door open and stepped inside, finding himself in a small but very dainty foyer. A decorative vase sat on the floor, against the wall. A gorgeous beach scene painting adorned most of the wall facing the doorway.

"Hello? Ma'am?"

Jack stepped through the foyer and to the adjoining den as he called out. There was no immediate answer as he took in the sight of the den. Everything in the place was immaculately cleaned. He could even smell faint traces of some sort of lemon-scented cleaner. The white couch looked so clean it could have passed for brand new. Every tabletop and picture frame seemed to shine. The appearance of the place suggested that either Madeline Holcomb did indeed have someone coming over to help her out around the house, or she was doing a lot of cleaning to deal with the stress she was going through.

He was so taken with the cleanliness of the place that it took him a moment to realize that he'd called out about five seconds ago and he hadn't gotten a response yet.

"Hello? Mrs. Holcomb? I'm an FBI agent, and I—"

"Would you just come to the damned bedroom?" that same voice called out from down a hallway off to the right of the den. "You know I can't hear you from out there!"

Jack grinned at the absolute fury in the woman's voice. Had this all been happening to someone else, he would have found it hilarious. The grin faltered when he realized that the woman clearly assumed him to be someone else. Based on his brief interaction with her so far, God only knew how she'd react when she discovered there was a stranger in her house. He didn't see her giving much of a damn if it was an FBI agent or not.

He walked down the hallway and found it just as clean as the foyer and the den. There were two large paintings on the walls—more beach scenes—and three small tables adorned with vases of fresh flowers along the length of it. He passed a small door he assumed was a closet and then passed an open room that was empty, a guest room from the looks of it. He assumed the woman's voice was coming from the bedroom at the end of the hallway. The door was opened, revealing half of a window, the curtains drawn to let the sunshine in.

"Ma'am, I'm an FBI agent," he said again, raising his voice this time. "My name is Agent Jack Rivers, and I've come by to check in on you."

"You're...what?"

He came to the doorway, knocked on the frame, and poked his head in. He'd approached many a door with caution and tact before, but this was a whole new experience.

He found a large master bedroom, just as clean as the rest of the house. The bed resting against the far wall looked to be Queen sized. Mrs. Madeline Holcomb was lying in it, under a single, thin sheet. She looked both aghast and pissed off when she saw an unfamiliar face look into her room. Her gray hair was done up in loose curls and from the appearance of her shoulders and neck, she was quite frail and thin.

"And who the hell do you think you are?" she yelled. Her face seemed to harden like stone and her thin, brittle lips formed a tight line.

"I tried telling you, ma'am. I'm Agent Jack Rivers with the FBI."

"FBI?"

"That's right. I'm in town working with the police on a case that we fear might very well be—"

"I thought you were my son! That's the only reason I told you to come in! If you don't show me some identification *right now*, we're going to have a problem."

"I do apologize," Jack said, fumbling for his ID. When he had it out, he walked closer to her, holding it out.

Madeline held out a hand, her fingers thin and wrinkled. "Stop right there!" She leaned forward and scrutinized his ID before eyeing him skeptically and giving a curt little nod.

"Again, I'm so sorry," Jack said, pocketing his ID. "But if you'll just let me explain…," he paused here, giving her the opportunity to interrupt again. When she did not, he continued. "There have been a series of murders in the city over the past few days and the only link we can find between them is that everyone victim was on a transplant list for a liver."

"What the hell?" She looked terrified at such a notion, going so far as to actually grip the sheet around her a bit tighter.

"Because your name is also on the list I'm here to see if you would object to police protection around your home until we have the killer in custody."

"You mean parked outside my house all day?"

"Yes ma'am. Not me personally, but a local Roanoke cop. And they'd only ever bother you or interrupt your day if they feel you're legitimately in danger."

She considered it for a moment, her eyes narrowing. "I don't see the point. My son is usually here to watch after me. Although, he is a good for nothing slouch most of the time. So maybe we *should* have a cop sit outside."

Jack found it peculiar that she'd talk about her son in such a way. It was apparent that someone was coming in to clean the place and take care of her. And from what he could tell, they were doing a very good job of it. If it was indeed her son, the guy should earn some sort of award for keeping the place so clean and putting up with this shit.

"Do you have any help?" he asked, trying to get clarification. "Is your son the only help you have?"

She seemed a little irritated by this question, letting out a deep sigh and rolling her eyes. "Yeah, he's the best I can do. I know the house is nice, but all my money is gone, you see. I suppose he does try very hard—as hard as he can, anyway—but it's always a struggle with him. He's far too lazy and has been for most of his damn life."

Slowly, little alarm bells started to ding inside of his head. The spotless house, the unappreciative mother that looked too weak to do anything on her own. There was something there for sure, but he couldn't quite make it fit.

"So here's what we'll do," he said, trying to make her feel as comfortable as possible, given that a stranger had just come into her home. "I'll go ahead and sit outside your house until a local policeman arrives. When your son shows up, we can also talk with him and get his thoughts on a police presence on the property."

"I say it's fine. He'd just make the wrong decision. He'd think he was more than man enough to stop danger." She gave a very dry laugh and said, "Like he could stop a murderer." She looked alarmed for the first time now, as if saying *murderer* had clued her into what was really going on.

"I'm very sorry to have disturbed you," Jack said. "I'll be out front, in my car. And you know…I just have to say, you have a lovely home. It's very clean, very crisp."

"Huh. You have my son to thank for that. It's the one thing he does that isn't completely useless. He cleans when he gets nervous…that type of *man.*"

"Do you know when your son will get back?" he asked, pressing for more information to see if his little tingle of intuition was right. "Does he have a job?"

"Yes, I guess you could call it a job. Some call-center bullshit. He tossed away a perfectly good life. Could have been a doctor. He started med school and…," she stopped and shrugged. "Then he started caring for me. I think he blames me for everything…how his life turned out."

It was the information about her son being an ex-medical student that sealed the deal for him. An unappreciative, sick mother. A son that was doing everything he could to make her comfortable—doing what he could to earn her approval. The way she spoke about him to a complete stranger spoke volumes, and it made Jack start to wonder just what lengths a son desperate for his mother's love and attention might go to.

"Well, he does a good job cleaning the house, that's for sure," he said. "What's his name, anyway? Just so I can let the cops know when he shows up."

"Brandon. He looks like a walking bundle of nerves, so you can't miss him."

"Well, you have a good day, Mrs. Holcomb."

She only gave a little nod as Jack made his way out of the room. He kept his cool as he walked through the hallway but was sprinting by the time he reached the den. He pulled out his phone on the way to the car and pulled up Rachel's number. It rang four times and kicked over to voicemail. Knowing that Rachel rarely checked her voice messages, he then sent a text.

Madeline Holcomb's son might be a fit. Brandon Holcomb. Call when you can.

With that done, he got into his car, not sure where to go. Rachel was likely at the hospital by now, but that felt like a bust. Maybe the best approach would be to head back to the station and see what he could find on Brandon Holcomb. Ah, but he had to stay here, stationed outside of the Holcomb residence until relief arrived.

He pulled out his phone again and this time called Stanhope. The deputy answered on the second ring, sounding like a frantic coach on the sidelines of a tight football game.

"Rivers?"

"Yeah, it's me. Look…I'm out here at Madeline Holcomb's house. I know you're stretched thin, but I could really use some relief here. I may have something of a lead I'd like to get behind."

"Give me a few minutes and I'll see what we can do. Anything I can do to help with that lead?"

"Yes, actually. I need to know as much as I can about Brandon Holcomb as soon as possible."

"I'll call the station and get someone on that right away. Hang tight, Agent Rivers. You'll be freed up soon enough."

Jack ended the call and found himself looking back to the Holcomb house. The hedges trimmed, the grass mowed pristinely, the inside sparkling clean. If it was all the work of Brandon Holcomb, it was clearly more than just trying to make his mother healthier and happier. He was trying to win her approval, despite the verbal abuse and tearing down.

And the more Jack thought about it, the more anxious he became…and as far as he was concerned, his relief could not get there soon enough.

CHAPTER TWENTY SEVEN

Rachel rushed to the front desk just inside the hospital's main doors. She already had her badge and ID pulled, fully prepared to deal with the legal hoops she'd likely have to jump through in order to get any information. On the drive over, she'd worked out a rather simple approach that wasn't quite a lie and she thought might work. The woman at the white, curved desk in the central lobby looked up with alarm as Rachel hurried over to her, flashing her ID.

"I'm Special Agent Rachel Gift," she said. "I need to know where a certain patient has been taken. He was just brought in within the last half an hour or so, I believe."

"And what's this in reg—"

"It's a matter of protection," she snapped. "We believe him to be in danger and I'll be stationed outside of his room until more local law enforcement arrive."

"Oh, oh, of course. What is the patient's name?"

"Seth Dillinger."

The woman typed the name into the laptop at her station and nodded almost right away. "Yes. He's been checked in and is currently in room 36C. Looks like he was moved there no more than five minutes ago."

Rachel took off at a sprint for the elevators. She still wasn't quite sure where the rush of certainty was coming from—a certainty that even though Dillinger was clearly not the killer at this point, there was something brewing here. Her mind kept going back to the idea that the killer had some sort of insider information. If he'd been able to get his hands on the transplant list, perhaps there was much more he could get. If he had some sort of connections, it wasn't even all that difficult to imagine him being able to know when someone was being rushed to the hospital. And perhaps most importantly, they'd also know that if a patient was rushed to the hospital and the situation was a life-or-death matter, that patient could very likely be ushed up the transplant list. And based on what they knew of the killer so far, that could very well be a trigger.

Rachel took the elevators up to the third floor and then took a right down the long hallway. As she neared Dillinger's room, she spotted a doctor and a nurse conversing not too far away from his room. She stopped alongside them, once again took out her ID, and introduced herself.

"I'm here to keep a check on Seth Dillinger. There's a very good chance he may be in danger. I'll be stationed outside of his room for a while, until local PD send someone to replace me. Can you give me an update?"

The doctor eyed her ID with heavy scrutiny before nodding slowly. "Is this really necessary?"

"I assure you it is." Then, lowering her voice, she said, "Three people have already been killed in the past five days—all of whom were on a transplant list. Someone at the hospital should have been called and—"

"Yes, yes, I'm so sorry. I do remember that memo going out." The doctor sighed heavily and have her a defeated nod. "That's fine. Now, will you need to speak with him?"

"That would be incredibly helpful. Is he coherent right now?"

"Yes. Well, perhaps. Given the situation, I'd allow it."

"And what about Mr. Dillinger? What can you tell me about his history?"

The doctor gave her another of his strained looks. She knew he was likely trying to figure out how much—if any—he should tell her based on the dichotomy of the doctor-patient relationship.

"Mr. Dillinger has had issues with his liver for several years, brought on by hepatitis. Right now, he is stable and receiving intravenous medicine to keep toxins out of his bloodstream. He'll likely be discharged in two or three days if his body responds well to the meds."

"But he *is* coherent right now?"

"Yes, but fairly weak. If you *must* speak with him, please keep it brief."

"Of course. Thank you."

She proceeded to 36C, her nerves now somewhat calmed. She supposed now that everyone willing to have police protection was covered, finding the killer would be significantly easier. Or maybe Dillinger himself would be able to offer her some information that would help them find the killer.

She knocked on the door and stepped inside the room. As she did, her phone buzzed a single time in her pocket, indicating she had a text. Even though she knew it could be one of several people (Jack, Paige's sitter, maybe even Peter, or someone tied to Alex Lynch) she ignored it for the moment. Right now, her full attention needed to be on Seth Dillinger.

"Mr. Dillinger?" she called as she stepped into the room.

She got a weak "Yeah?" in response.

She entered the room and found a man of about forty or so laying in bed. He had brown hair and eyes, the hair hanging mostly over his brow. A ragged-looking beard wasn't quite fully grown in, showing about a week's worth of growth. An IV had been placed into his left arm. He looked very tired and clearly unhappy to be in the hospital.

"Mr. Dillinger, my name is Rachel Gift. I'm a special agent with the FBI. I understand you've had a very active morning, so I'll make this quick."

"FBI? What…um ok. What's going on?"

"Over the last few days, three people have been killed and they are all on the transplant list for a liver. I came to your house this morning to warn you about this and to question you but found that you'd had a turn for the worse."

"That's for sure. It's my own damned fault, though. I wasn't the best about taking my meds regularly. But…for real? There's someone killing people on the transplant list?"

"It seems that way. Currently the local police are contacting each person and asking if they'd be okay with police protection until the matter is solved."

"Oh. Well…," he stopped and gestured around at the room. "Seems like I'm in a pretty safe place for now, right?"

"All the same, we'll likely have someone stationed outside of your room for the next day or so. I just thought you'd want to know."

He shrugged, but it was evident by his expression that he wasn't the biggest fan of this idea. "Fine by me." He grinned at her in a sleepy sort of way, one she thought might have come off as flirtatious if he wasn't so weary. "Feel free to poke your head back in every now and then. You'd likely be the only visitor I get."

Ignoring this, Rachel sidestepped to one final course of conversation. "Mr. Dillinger, in the time that you've been ill, has there ever been anyone that has approached you in a negative way?"

"No one that sticks out, no. I mean, I have a pretty shady past, I'll admit. I'm sure some might see what's happened to me over the past few years as a form of karma or whatever, but—"

The door opened behind them, and Rachel watched as a nurse entered. It was a male nurse, wearing a smile on his face, the same sort of smile Rachel assumed most nurses wore when they met a new patient for the first time. He looked from Dillinger and then to Rachel, confused.

"Oh, I'm so sorry. I didn't know he already had a visitor."

"It's okay," Rachel said. "Just give us one more moment, would you?"

The nurse nodded rather nervously and the way he flinched away when he gave Rachel a quick once-over made her take notice. When his eyes saw her holstered Glock on her waist, his eyes went wide for just a moment, but he kept his composure. She understood it, she supposed; the last thing a nurse expected to see in the room of their patient was an armed visitor.

"FBI," Rachel explained almost apologetically.

"Ah, yes, okay."

Again, his eyes trailed to her gun, and she was quite sure she saw a flicker of fear in his eyes when she'd mentioned that she was with the FBI. When he started making his way over to Dillinger, he looked a little shaken. He'd come in confident but now, after having found a visitor already in the room and then seeing her weapon, he was flustered. Not just that, he was scared. His scrubs looked clean and fresh. Something was settled down in his right pants pocket, something shiny that barely stuck out of the pocket. Below that, she noticed that he wore a pair of cheap-looking sneakers. They weren't filthy by any means, but there were signs of dirt on them. More than that, they didn't look comfortable at all. Didn't most nurses wear very comfortable shoes, some even resorting to those weird-looking Croc shoes?

"Sir?" Rachel said. "Can I please get your name?"

He took another step toward the side of Dillinger's bed. His hand briefly started to lift up to the pocket with the shiny thing in it. It was curved at the top, and a dull silver in color. By the time Rachel thought it might be a scalpel, the man took one more huge stride toward Dillinger.

"No, stop right there," Rachel demanded.

The nurse let out a little moan, his face scrunching up. And in a flash so fast that Rachel hardly even saw it, he raced to the end of the bed heading for the door. Rachel took a hard sprint to cut him off but missed him by about half a second. When she redirected, she saw that he was already at the door, pulling it open and rushing out into the hallway.

Rachel gave one final glance to Seth Dillinger and followed after him.

CHAPTER TWENTY EIGHT

When she came out into the hallway, the nurse that had been speaking with the doctor earlier was still standing at her station, behind one of the mobile computer units on wheels. She was already looking down the hall with wide, alarmed eyes. When she saw Rachel, she pointed to the end of the hall. "That way," she said.

Rachel sprinted towards the end of the hall, where it ended and offered only a left turn. As she raced in that direction, she heard a shout of complaint from up ahead, hidden by the wall. Hurrying in that direction, she was vaguely aware of her phone dinging in her pocket again. But that may as well have been happening on some other planet because for right now, she was hyper-focused on catching the male nurse.

She came to the bend in the hallway and took the left. A handful of nurses and other employees were all looking further down the hall, huddled together and trying to figure out what was going on. Rachel looked that way and saw a stairwell doorway slowly closing on its own. Without asking any questions, she rushed to the door. When she opened it back up and passed through it, she reached for her sidearm. She'd much rather not use it in a hospital, but she reminded herself that the nurse had a scalpel in one of his pockets.

He'd come in to kill Dillinger, she thought. *But then the unexpected appearance of an armed FBI agent clearly spooked them and now they're on the run. Now they—*

She stepped through the doorway and was greeted with a hard right hand to the shoulder. It clipped her shoulder bone, making her think it had been intended for her face. She staggered backwards, directly into the door, and saw the nurse right in front of her. He hesitated as he reached for the shining thing in his pocket—a scalpel from what Rachel could tell.

Rachel drew her arm back to retaliate and that seemed to send the nurse into overdrive. He started for the stairs, going so fast that he nearly fell down the first flight. He caught himself on the metal rail and tumbled down the rest of the flight.

Rachel chased him right away, getting so close as they came to the first landing that when she reached out to grab him, her fingertips grazed the back of his scrubs. In reaching, Rachel missed a stair and stumbled a bit herself. She held her hands out to keep from slamming into the landing wall, giving the nurse another head-start on her. As she rebounded from the wall, she saw that he was somehow already down the next flight. She briefly looked down through the maze of rails that descended toward the first floor. She could hear hurried footfalls, and then another door opening up somewhere. Rachel started racing down the flight, coming to the landing for the second floor and then stopped.

"Shit," she said.

The way the man had run, taking that immediate left and then knowing where the stairwells were…it was odd. He'd hurried through it all with the speed and confidence of a man that knew where he was going. It seemed her preliminary hunch was at least somewhat correct: he had familiarity with this hospital. And that meant he would be able to outsmart her. More than that, he'd successfully led her away from Dillinger's room. She'd done exactly what he'd hoped for.

Rachel stopped as she made her way down the second-floor stairs. *Maybe he knows,* she thought. *Maybe he's figured out that everyone on the list is being watched now and he's desperate to get to Dillinger. And I've been pulled right away from the damned room…*

Angry with herself, she turned around and rushed back up the stairs. If he was expecting her to follow him while he still had a sizeable lead, he was going to be sorely mistaken. She'd get back to the room and give an order for the place to be put on lockdown. If she could manage that, then she—

Blinding pain tore through her head. It came out of nowhere and for a dreadful moment, she thought maybe the nurse was still here in the stairwell and had stabbed her in the back of the head. *That's* how intense the pain was.

She shouted out in surprise and pain as she was in mid-step. She fell slightly down the stairs, losing her balance and falling back to the landing between floors. It was only a three-foot drop, but enough to send a flare of pain from her butt bone upwards and knocking the breath out of her. But that little pain was nothing compared to the juggernaut roaring in her head.

Little black stars zipped across her field of vision. Creeping dark blurs started to come in at the corners of her eyes and pulsed. It felt as if a pair of massive hands were gripping her head and trying to literally rip her skull apart. She gasped in little hitched breaths, as she still had not managed to get her wind back from the fall.

No. Not now…not now…

The pain roared back and when it did, Rachel worried that this was it. The little episodes that had come before had been warnings, but this was the real deal. Maybe she died here, in this dark stairwell. Maybe she wouldn't stop the killer, or ever see Paige again, or…

She slowly got to her feet and made herself take a series of small breaths. Her legs were shaky, and the stairs seemed to move and shift all around her. She wanted to shout out, not for help but to tell someone to keep an eye on Dillinger's room, for someone to lock the building down in the event the killer tried to escape. But she couldn't draw in enough breath. It was hard enough to simply breathe, the pain in her head seeming to rob her of every single ounce of breath and energy inside of her.

Slowly, she made her way back up the stairs. One by one, she forced her feet to remember what they were designed to do. The stairs still seemed like living, breathing creatures, but she managed to make it up them.

"Someone," she said, trying to yell. But even the act of speaking seemed to make the pain worse. "Someone…please…"

She gripped the railing tightly as she tried to take a breath while lifting a foot and then releasing it when she set the foot down on the next step. Realizing that she may be in a very bad spot here, Rachel dug her phone out of her pocket with the intentions of texting Jack. If nothing else, he could call and have the place put on lockdown. But right now, the idea of hurrying up the stairs and doing it herself felt far too hard.

With her phone in her hand as she took another stair upwards, she saw that she'd missed two texts from Jack. The first one read: *Madeline Holcomb's son might be a fit. Brandon Holcomb. Call when you can.* The words were surprisingly crisp in her vision, and she found that by concentrating on them, the black streaks and pulsing edges around her vision seemed to fade.

The second read: *Answer your phone! B. Holcomb was a former volunteer at Roanoke General and his mother is on the list. Could be at the hospital right now!*

And Rachel would bet anything that he was currently wearing a pair of new-looking scrubs, dirty shoes, and carrying a scalpel in his pocket.

She closed her eyes and took a very deep breath. She texted back after opening her eyes, relieved that she could move her fingers without much of a problem. But the letters swam in front of her, some of them highlighted by the thin, blazing strips that darted across her eyes. And as she focused on the message she was composing, she found that the pain in her head was starting to fade. It went from a massive explosion of anguish to a very bad migraine swarming her head like a nest of bees. And by the time she'd typed out: *I'm there now and unable to do much. Have them go to lock-down,* it had downgraded to an irritating ache right behind her eyes.

She pocketed her phone and took a few more careful steps up. By the time she was at the top of the landing and reaching for the door that would open back up to the third floor, it was almost back to normal. There were a few stubborn black stars cascading across her vision and she felt like she had a minor case of vertigo but that was all.

That's all? she told herself. *Don't you dare forget about that pain. You can still feel it in your stomach, can't you? It took your breath. And it's getting worse every single time it happens. Don't you dare ign—*

She opened the door and stepped out into the third-floor hallway. The lights seemed impossibly bright at first and the flurry of motion that came in the presence of moving people made that slight dizziness a bit worse for a moment. But she stood still, allowing herself just a moment to let her body recalibrate. She then stepped forward, and then took another step. When she trusted her legs and feet to carry her, she hurried to the place in the hallway where she'd taken the left before— which was now a right from her point of view—she heard a slight commotion from up ahead. This included a familiar voice that made no sense at first. But as she hurried to the corner and took the turn back towards room 36C, she saw the face that matched the voice, and an instant swarm of relief came over her.

It was Jack. He was speaking in a near-shout to a pair of people behind the nurse's station on the right-hand wall in the center of the hallway. "...and can take it up with the police Captain, but right now, I need you to shut down the place! We have a potential killer and—"

It was then that he saw Rachel. She was heading in his direction but already angling for room 36C. "Jack...go...no time!"

He hurried over to her, concern on his face. "Rachel, what the hell is wrong? You're sweating and pale. Are you—"

"He was here," she said "I saw him and he—"

An abrupt curse word from up ahead interrupted her. It was soft and muffled, coming from behind the closed door of 36C. Without another word exchanged between them, they went for the door. Jack took the lead, entering the room slowly. His gun was drawn but his stride was slow, unsure of what to expect. Rachel followed close behind. She did not draw her Glock just yet but had her hand hovering over the butt.

She stepped into view of the bed just as Jack started to speak. She saw that several of her hunches had been correct. The man—presumably Brandon Holcomb—had indeed come circling back around to make his way back to Dillinger's room. He stood by the head of the bed, currently holding a scalpel in his right hand. Seth Dillinger had managed to block an attack, both of his arms blocking Holcomb's right arm. The IV was stretched tight from the motion, and Dillinger's arms were shaking.

Worse yet, Rachel and Jack entering distracted both men. Dillinger's grip slipped from Holcomb's wrist and the scalpel came down. However, Brandon Holcomb did not attack right away He hesitated, holding the scalpel to Dillinger's neck. His hands were trembling and as they watched, Rachel could see a small bead of blood seep out of a minor cut on Dillinger's neck.

"Don't do it," Rachel gasped. "Not...worth it."

"Oh yes it is," Holcomb cried out. "I have to help. She needs my help and if I don't, she won't stop...her voice...it won't...."

"Brandon, right?" Jack said, looking at the man with the scalpel. "Brandon Holcomb?"

The man looked amazed that Jack had said his name but also shook his head slowly. "Yeah, that's me."

"I need you to drop that scalpel. I'm not sure what you're up to, exactly. But I need you to drop it."

"You have to let me do this. I have to..."

"For your mother, right?"

Again, he gave that amazed expression. This time, though, at the mention of his mother, he withdrew his arm. Rachel watched closely, ready to draw and fire if he decided to make any sudden movements with that arm. But it hung listlessly by his side, the scalpel all but forgotten for the moment.

"How do you know about my mother?" he asked, his voice low and desperate.

"I spoke with her. Not too long ago."

"How?" His hands continued to shake. Rachel's hand slowly went for the butt of her gun because if that shaking continued, she thought Dillinger's throat might get cut completely by accident.

"Brandon...the things you've been doing lately aren't helping her. I know you think it might be, but—"

"Of course it is!" The scalpel came back up, but it did not point in any particular direction. It was almost as if he just wanted to remind them that he had it. "She's the only one that deserves to be on the list!"

"And this man doesn't?" Jack asked.

Rachel kept her hand just above her gun. She was rather hoping that with Jack engaging the man in such a direct way, she'd become nothing more than a shape in the background. She was fully prepared to draw her weapon, but her body was still reeling from her moment of extreme weakness in the stairwell. Even as she stood there in the hospital room, her knees didn't quite feel fully there.

"You're a cop?" Holcomb asked.

"FBI," Jack answered.

"Then you know this man is a sex offender, right?"

"That's bullshit!" Dillinger said. "It was one time, when I—"

"Zip it, Mr. Dillinger," Jack said. "Now is not the time."

"He's no good," Holcomb went on. "And if I kill him, *everyone* moves up the list. Not just my mother. Everyone."

Something dark and barbed stirred within Rachel when she realized there was a bit of logic to this point. She recalled Dillinger telling her he was lax about taking his meds. And this was apparently a common problem with Dillinger. Was he terminal? Was his a lost case? Maybe taking him out of the list *would* help others.

That's got to be the tumor talking, Rachel thought. As if in response, she felt a tremor in her head, an echo of the horrendous pain she'd felt while down in the stairwell.

"Listen to me, Mr. Holcomb," Jack said. "If you don't drop that scalpel and step away from the bed, I'm going to have to shoot. You understand that, right?"

"But I have to. I have to make her happy…I have to save her."

Rachel could tell by the growing confidence and yearning in Brandon Holcomb's eyes that he wasn't going to back down. He had no intention of letting his mother down. And he would be willing to take a bullet in order to take this step.

A crazy idea came to her and when it locked itself in place, she felt tears stinging at her eyes. Before she could change her mind or talk herself out of it, she opened her mouth and started talking.

And by then, it was too late to take it back.

CHAPTER TWENTY SEVEN

"I hope you know we don't want to shoot you," Rachel said. "In fact, we don't want anyone else to get killed. No one else has to die. I know your mom must be scared...just like this man in the bed. And I know what that fright feels like. You see, Mr. Holcomb, I'm dying, too."

There. There it was. Out in the open. As the words came out of her mouth, it felt like a huge river of poison came flowing out of her— poison that had been pooling up and collecting around her heart, coming out in the form of words. In the form of confession.

"Don't lie to me!" It was clear he thought she was simply trying to give him some fake sympathy, trying to connect with him. But Rachel thought she also saw a softening in his eyes. She recalled the way she'd originally felt when she'd read Joseph Quinn's story—about how he knew loss just like the family he'd had to deliver that awful news to.

She saw that in Brandon Holcomb. In his eyes, she saw the *hope* that someone else might have at least some sort of glimmer of what he was dealing with.

"I'm not telling lies," she said. "I'm dying from something pretty harsh. There's no transplant list to save me...nothing I can look to in order to make it better. There's chemo, but I'm not wasting the last bit of my life on being sick. I know the fear, Mr. Holcomb. But I think I can also say with a degree of certainty that I wouldn't want anyone else to die just so I *might* stand a better chance of living. Are you sure this is what your mother would want?"

She saw some of the confidence leave his eyes. She was also vaguely aware of Jack standing to her left, just ahead of her. He'd not yet turned back to look at her, but she could only imagine what he must be thinking. As far as she knew, he might think she was telling lies to distract Holcomb. Truth be told, it would be an effective method.

"I hear her when she's not even there," Holcomb said. The scalpel lowered again. Less than a foot away from him, Seth Dillinger leaned hard to the left side of the bed. He was nearly sitting up, the IV still attached as he did his best to stay away from being stabbed.

"You're trying to please her, right?" Rachel asked.

Holcomb only nodded. A single tear came out of his left eye and trailed down the side of his face.

"Does she know you're doing this? Three people already…does she know?"

Holcomb shook his head. "But there are less people on the list now…because of what I've done. She'll have a better chance."

There's a confession, without really even trying, Rachel thought. But before getting too distracted, she went on. She knew she had the hook in. Now all she had to do was reel him in.

"Like I said, I know the fear. But I have to think she would not want you hurting people just to give her hope. Do you think that's really—"

Jack moved so quickly and unexpectedly that the suddenness of it even had Rachel take a quick step back. He took a big lunge forward and slammed a fist directly into Holcomb's solar plexus. Holcomb went stumbling back into the wall behind the bed and though he did make an effort to slash out at Seth Dillinger, Jack blocked it easily.

Jack grabbed Holcomb's right wrist and bent it back fiercely. Holcomb cried out and was only able to hold on to the scalpel for a few seconds. His fingers opened up as he did his best to get out of Jack's grip, and the scalpel went clattering to the floor. After that, Rachel thought she could literally see the fight and the will drain right out of Brandon Holcomb. Jack spun him around so that his face pressed directly into the wall and then pulled his arms behind him to apply handcuffs. Holcomb fought only the slightest bit but by the time the cuffs snapped into place, he had started crying softly against the wall.

Rachel started forward to see if she could assist in any way. Jack apparently caught sight of her motion out of the corner of his eyes because without even turning his head, he said, "Let a doctor know we're good here. And that they may need to check on Mr. Dillinger."

It was incredibly rare for Jack to give such blatant instructions to her, so it sounded a bit jarring. But Rachel did as he'd asked, heading out into the hallway. There were a few people standing around outside of the door, clearly having been listening to all that had been transpiring in the room 36C.

"Someone needs to check on the patient," she said. "And it's okay to call off the lock-down. The suspect has been apprehended."

"Hey, Gift!"

She turned and saw Stanhope rushing down the hall. He moved swiftly, but it was evident that he was not used to moving so fast. "Everything okay?"

"Yes," she said as Stanhope approached her, breathing heavily. "Agent Rivers has Brandon Holcomb disarmed and handcuffed inside."

"Good, good. Great work. They...hold on." He studied her face for a moment and frowned slightly. "You look a little rattled, Gift. You okay?"

She thought of the moment she'd had in the stairwell—the worst episode she'd suffered ever since the first one out on the training course in Richmond—the one that had convinced her to go to the doctor. The memory of blacking out on the course and the immense pain she'd felt in the stairwell stuck to the forefront of her mind and would not release. Still, she managed to give a quick nod of her head. The smile she offered was a bit harder to create.

"Yes, I'm good."

Together, they walked into 36C. Two nurses had already hurried in and were checking Seth Dillinger's vitals. Jack still stood with Brandon Holcomb, slowly guiding him away from the bed and toward the door.

"Deputy Stanhope," Jack said. "I'm sorry to do this to you, but would you mind escorting Mr. Holcomb out of the hospital and giving him a ride to the station. I need to discuss something with Agent Gift for a second."

"Sure thing" he seemed to have caught his breath as he swapped places with Jack. "Anything else I can do?"

"I think we're good for now," Rachel said.

Jack looked to her and she saw an emotion in his eyes that she could not quite read. But when he passed by her and spoke two simple words to her, she thought she recognized that emotion as fear.

"Come on," he said, marching out of the room without bothering to look behind him.

***

They sat on a wooden bench in the small garden area to the right of the hospital. The garden was nothing special, just a thin trail that wound through a thin grove of trees and passed by a flowerbed in need of a good weeding. Afternoon had set in, and the sun beat down on them gently.

"Is it true?" Jack asked.

She thought it would be harder to answer, but it came out easy. She supposed her admission in room 36C had been the equivalent of pulling off a band-aid and now the rest wasn't going to be as painful.

"Yes, it's true."

141

Jack hung his head and looked to the ground. Rachel felt that she knew him well, but she had no idea how he would react. Would he be mad because she'd kept it from him? Would he be saddened to have to accept the fact that she was going to die? Or…and this was the one she was really interested in, would he try to talk her into doing whatever was possible to increase her odds of beating her cancer?

"How long have you known?" he asked with a soft tone.

"Nearly a month now."

He didn't turn to fully look at her, but his eyes turned in her direction. "And you've been working as if nothing was wrong?"

"I have. I don't know if you can understand this, but I sort of had to."

"Does your family know?"

"Peter does. I just told him a few days ago."

He looked off in the direction of the path that led into the trees. She followed his gaze and wondered if maybe she could go hide there for a while…a day, a month, however much longer she had left.

"I told you that you looked sweaty and pale when we met in the hallway upstairs. Had something happened?"

"Yeah. I have these…these *episodes* sometimes and—"

"Wait, hold on," he sounded angry for the first time as he looked her directly in the eyes. "So when you told me about your grandmother being sick, you were telling me lies? It was you the whole time?"

"No, actually. Believe it or not, my grandmother has cancer, too. Breast cancer, and it's pretty advanced. She told me not long after I found out." She shrugged and, doing her very best to make light of the situation, added: "Talk about your ultimate double-whammy, huh?"

"You can't keep coming to work."

"I know. I figure one or two more cases and then I'm out."

"How about zero more cases?"

She shook her head and the next words that came out of her mouth were a hard, bitter truth. "I can't. I need to work."

"Why? What can't you face by yourself at home?"

She knew the answer, though she had never been able to admit it to herself. She confessed it in her mind in that moment but didn't dare speak it out loud. She had to work because it allowed her to run away from her fear of failure. She'd always been phenomenal at work. At home, she'd always felt like a sub par mother and wife. Especially now with the way everything had happened.

"Rachel, if Anderson finds out you kept this from him…"

"He won't. You have my word on this, Jack. One or two more cases. Or if one of these little episodes just takes all of the wind out of my sails."

"Do you know...how much time do you have left?"

"About a year."

"Jesus, Rachel."

There was a gasp in his voice as he said it. He reached out and took her hand and she let him. There was nothing romantic or forward in it. They'd placed their lives in the hands of the other far too many times for a gesture of such encouragement and sorrow to be misconstrued as anything it wasn't meant to be.

"I'll um....," Jack started to say. He stopped and wiped a tear from his eye before it had a chance to fall. He cleared his throat and started again. "I'll do whatever you need, Rachel. I'll *be* whatever you need. But I have to tell you this, as your friend...not your partner. If you keep working with this and I see that it's affecting you and putting you in even more danger, I'm going to call you out on it. And at that point, you'll either tell Anderson, or I will. Agreed?"

Fighting back tears of her own, Rachel squeezed is hand. "Agreed."

Neither of them said another word, though they continued sneaking glances toward the front of the hospital, waiting to see Stanhope come out with Brandon Holcomb in tow. In the meantime, they sat in the warmth of the afternoon among flowers and a few buzzing bees as Rachel slowly started to realize that the more she talked about her condition, the better she felt. She was afraid of what that meant, but in that one almost-perfect moment, she was more than willing to take it on.

CHAPTER TWENTY EIGHT

Rachel wasn't sure if it was the moment she'd shared with Jack in the hospital garden or the scare she'd had in the hospital stairwell, but she opted not to take part in the interrogation of Brendan Holcomb. Jack and Stanhope teamed up on it while Rachel sat at their temporary cubicle space and started writing up a report for Anderson.

The beats and events of the case came easily enough, and she had never minded the act of writing a report, but she found this one painstaking. When she realized that it just wasn't going to happen, she checked the time on her phone. When she saw that it had somehow come to be 5:40, she didn't hesitate at all. She called the sitter's number, almost opting for a plain voice call rather than FaceTime, mainly because Paige's little voice could be so loud. But, no, she wanted to see her kiddo's face. Besides, the room with the cubicles was pretty much empty.

Paige answered on the third ring, with the screen aimed directly at her nose. Currently, it showed a close-up of her nostrils. "Do you see my boogers, Mommy?"

The laughter that burst out of Rachel was genuine. She got control over it after three seconds or so, biting at her lip to keep it in.

"I do," she said. "There's quite a few bats in those caves."

"Eeew," Paige squealed. "You coming home soon, Mommy?"

"I am! In fact, just as soon as Mr. Jack is done speaking to someone, we're going to leave and head back home. It might be later tonight, but I *will* be home. If I don't see you before bedtime tonight, I'll be there in the house when you wake up."

She didn't realize until after she'd said this that it might not be accurate. After Peter's decision to separate and to be the one to primarily care for Paige for a while, she wasn't sure if sleeping in their home was the best idea. If she had to, though, she'd sleep on the damned couch.

"That's awesome," Paige said. "Daddy said he's bringing burgers from Five Guys for dinner tonight. Want me to save you some fries?"

"Of course I do. Are you being good?"

"Yeah! I always am."

"I know you are."

144

She stopped here, realizing she was out of things to say and that she was about to start crying. She had to tell Paige. Somehow, she was going to have to tell her daughter that she had about one year left to live.

"Okay, go get back to your homework."

"I already did my homework. I'm working on some melty beads right now."

"Oh no. You better not have them all over the carpet." She had to get off *now* or Paige was going to see her cry over FaceTime.

"I won't."

"Okay. Bye, Paige."

She hung up, the screen momentarily freezing on Paige's wide smile. She set the phone down gently and wondered how in the hell she was supposed to tell her eight-year-old daughter that she was going to die. The sad part of it was that she'd need Peter to help. He'd always done exceptionally well with translating difficult topics into kidspeak.

As she was caught up in trying to sort this out, she heard voices approaching. Jack's was easy enough, and Stanhope's deep timbre was also hard to miss. They were coming into the large workroom, coming around to her side of the wall of cubicles. When they stepped into view, Stanhope looked pleased, but tired. Jack looked rather drained, but there was an unmistakable look of satisfaction on his face—the look of a man that believed he'd just wrapped up a job well done.

"Well," Jack said, "I know he all but confessed in the hospital room, but we got a solid one just now. A confession and more, really."

"You weren't even in there for half an hour," she pointed out.

Stanhope sighed, resting his backside on the edge of Rachel's borrowed desk. "That poor bastard has wanted to get everything out for ages, it seemed."

"Once he started, it just wouldn't stop," Jack said. "And I met his mother for a bit today, so I at least have a reference point. She was always tearing him down, talking bad about him. I think it just drove him to do whatever it took to please her. He had started med school about twelve years ago, but his mom got sick and there was no father or other family around, so it was all on him. He dropped out, took on some menial jobs and did his best to care for her. But they were always broke because of medicine and hospital stays. Mom directed her anger and disappointment at him—something he says she's been doing since he was just a kid. She blames him for her husband leaving, for why she had no social life, for why they were always struggling."

"My God," Rachel said. "And all he wanted to do was make her happy?"

"Yeah. He thought by making sure she got to the top of that transplant list, she'd be healthier. But he also claims to have heard her voice in his head. Not like recalling things she'd said, but as if she were with him all the time. So, I think there's a mental illness aspect to it, too. A psychiatrist is coming in to see him within the hour."

"Was she actually sending him out to kill people?"

"Not according to him," Stanhope said. "He swears up and down that his mother had no idea what he was up to."

The trio fell into silence for several tense moments as the weight of the case settled on them. These were the sorts of cases that truly got under Rachel's skin. She'd much rather deal with someone that had very pointed and violent motives rather than someone that had gone to such lengths just because they felt unseen and unheard.

"Deputy Stanhope, it was a pleasure working with you," she said, getting to her feet. "But if it's all the same to you, I'd really like to get home to my daughter before she goes to sleep."

"Oh, I have two of my own. I know how important the bedtime routine is, so don't let me stop you. I'll just email over any paperwork that pops up."

He gave them a pleasant wave and shook their hands before heading off elsewhere into the building. Jack looked to Rachel, as if considering something. "How are you feeling?"

"Surprisingly fine. I dreaded telling you everything but now that it's out…yeah. It feels better."

"When do you think you'll tell Paige?"

"I'm still not quite sure," she said, cleaning up the papers they'd accumulated during their time at the station. She thought of Brandon Holcomb, so badly wanting his mother's attention and approval that he'd resorted to murder. All he'd wanted was to be heard and respected. Catching a little tear at the corner of her eye, she added: "Sooner rather than later, though."

CHAPTER TWENTY NINE

Rachel looked to the couch where she'd slept the night before, wondering if it was obvious that it had been used as a bed for the past two nights. She'd straightened it up as well as she could and thought she'd hidden it well. It was likely not anything Paige would notice, but she thought Grandma Tate would. And seeing as how Grandma Tate was due to call at any moment, Rachel was on high alert. She straightened up the blanket she'd folded and tossed strategically on the corner of the armrest.

Paige sat beside her, looking through several pieces of artwork she'd done at school. She was excited to show each one of them to Grandma Tate and was sorting them out in order from her favorite to least favorite.

When the iPad on the coffee table started ringing, Paige leaned forward to answer it so fast that she nearly dropped every piece of art to the floor. She managed to snag them at the last minute while also answering the FaceTime call.

"Hey, Gramma!"

Grandma Tate smiled widely into the camera. The woman never had to fake a smile for Paige, that was for sure. Her face always lit up when she saw her great-granddaughter. Sometimes, like today, it was the kind of smile that made her look nearly a decade younger.

"Hey yourself, Ms. Paige! How are you?"

"I'm good!"

"And your mom?"

Rachel leaned over, trying to get into the screen the slightest little bit while Paige continued to insist her face should be front and center—which was usually the way these calls went. "Yea, I'm here, too. And I'm good."

"Hey, you wanna see an art show?" Paige asked.

"What sort of art show?"

Rachel leaned back, feeling silly for having worried about Grandma Tate noticing the state of the couch. As she watched Paige shove paper after paper in front of the iPad, she wondered how much longer she'd be sleeping on the couch. On the night she'd come back from Roanoke, she'd been fully prepared for Peter to demand she head out for a hotel.

Instead, he'd offered to sleep in the couch, but she'd insisted on taking it.

Since then, they'd spoken maybe three sentences to one another. And the unspoken understanding so far was that she was fine to stay here for a while until they figured out some way to tell Paige everything—the looming separation as well as her health diagnosis—but she'd be sleeping on the couch.

It took about three minutes for Paige to get through her art show, the final piece titled *Monkey Rides Lion,* according to Paige. Rachel couldn't help but smile at the interaction between the two of them. It was also hard to believe just how vibrant Grandma Tate seemed. It was hard to believe she was living with a cancer that would likely take her out pretty swiftly.

"You're looking good, Grandma," she said.

"Well, thank you. It's been a long evening, though, I'll tell you that."

"How so? Is everything okay?"

Paige, apparently sensing adult-talk coming on, got down from the couch and went off in search of other things to show off.

"Yeah. I don't know if you remember Deborah Wilkes...an old friend of mine that used to be very close to the family?"

"The name rings a bell, sure."

"Well, as you may or may not know, we had a falling out about twenty years ago, right around the holidays. It got pretty nasty, and we haven't spoken since. It never really sat right with me, you know? And with things going the way they are...," She stopped here, shrugged and finished, "I called her up today. After almost twenty years. It was tense and it was weird, but I'm so very glad I did it."

"Did you...did you tell her your news?"

"No. Between you and me...yes, I called her because my days are numbered, and I don't want to leave any old, wilted relationships to die in a negative light. But I couldn't very well tell *her* that, right? It would seem sort of selfish. I just...well, I'm becoming very aware that I don't want to leave anything unsaid. And just so you know, that may involve a call to your father."

It wasn't even his *name,* but the mention of her father stung her heart. But it also raised an issue that she hadn't even considered in years.

"My father?" she said. She looked up to see if Paige was still there, but she was currently in the hallway, likely headed to the stairs to find something in her room to show Grandma Tate. "You know how to reach him?"

"Yes. I have for a few years now. I never mentioned it because I didn't think you'd care."

She almost said, *"I don't."* But she was still hanging onto what Grandma Tate had just said to her. *I don't want to leave any old, wilted relationships to die in a negative light...I don't want to leave anything unsaid.*

"Would you...," Jesus, she couldn't say it.

"Yes, dear?"

"Would you be willing to tell me how to get in touch with him?"

"Oh, Rachel. Don't let my last-minute missions before death rub off on you. These are things I need to do. It shouldn't affect you."

"I know, but...the idea of losing you has sort of opened up a lot." It wasn't a lie, but it wasn't what she truly wanted to say. It dawned on her then that maybe at some point, she'd have to tell Grandma Tate about her tumor, too. God, why did it all feel so complicated.

"If that's really what you want, let's wait until after I speak to him. It may be a bad idea, after all. Let me talk to him first and then we'll see."

Rachel could only nod. She hadn't even entertained the idea of trying to find and speak to her father in a handful of years. The idea seemed new and just as dangerous as ever. Her mother would be discussed, and a very heated argument would occur. Blame would be assigned, and names would be called, and it was not something she wanted to revisit. It was why she'd all but convinced herself that her father had simply winked out of existence nearly a decade ago.

She opened her mouth to speak but then heard Paige coming back down the stairs, her rapid footfalls like that of one hundred ponies.

"She needs to see the princess crown I made with melty beads!"

"You're right!" Rachel said, far too relieved to have been so forcefully removed from the sudden seriousness of the conversation.

Paige hopped back up onto the couch, taking her spot back. Rachel once again resigned herself to the outskirts of the camera frame as Paige showed off her newest melty-bead creation. "Yeah, and Daddy even let me use the iron for them this time," she bragged as she filled the screen with the plastic crown.

Rachel felt blindsided. She'd gone from not having thought of her father in several days—and not even thinking of trying to locate and talk to him in years—to now resting on the certainty that she needed to do that very thing sometime soon. Because she *did* have very few days left. And if she continued to work the way she was, even that year the doctor had given her may not be an accurate timeframe.

She continued to listen to Paige and Grandma Tate talk, smiling in all the right places and responding to questions or comments when appropriate. But the entire time, her thoughts were on her father—a ghost that had not haunted her mind in a very long time. And now that she knew her days were numbered, he seemed to suddenly be rattling his chains a little louder than he had in the past.

***

The following day, one hour before she was due to pick Paige up from school, Rachel met Jack at a coffee shop. Rachel had not yet returned to work, having called in sick with the excuse of migraines. Coming off of yet another successful closed case, no one had really batted an eye. Jack had gone back to work as usual, though, taking something of an extended lunch break to meet with her. They'd not spoken since parting ways after returning home from Roanoke and even though there had been no arguments or cross words between them, this was a conversation Rachel was dreading.

He started the conversation bluntly enough, but not in a harsh or critical way. He sat down across from her, coffee in hand, and asked: "Did you tell Paige yet?"

"No, not yet."

He frowned but nodded. "Can I ask why? I mean, I have no children, so I can't even imagine what breaking this sort of news must be like. But I also can't see how it's good to keep it in."

"The easy answer is 'because I'm a coward.' The more complicated answer has to do with her being eight years old and not fully understanding the gravity of it. It's a strange age, you know?"

"And what about Peter? Has he been supportive?"

"He's checked out. He's threatening to leave me."

"What?"

She shrugged, wishing she hadn't said it. But damn it, she had to tell someone, didn't she? "He's pissed—and understandably so—that I not only waited so long to tell him, but because I'm not interested in getting treatment."

"Like chemo?" And then, as if still hung up on it, he shook his head and said, "Really? He'd leave you over this?"

"Yes, like chemo," she said. "I just can't see going through all of that sickness and weakness when there isn't even a solid guarantee that

I'll come out the other side cancer-free. Based on what the doctor has told me, we've caught it late. Not late enough where there's *no* hope, but there's at least *some.*

"And it's more than the sickness. There's the fact that I went to Alex Lynch for help without telling him—or anyone, really—and the trouble it's caused. It's also the fact that I chose work over family right away, even in the midst of all of it and..."

She trailed off, starting to feel entirely too ashamed of herself.

"You know, it's funny you mentioned *some hope*," he said with a sly smile. He dug into his pocket and pulled out a business card. He slid it over to her slowly, as if he might take it back at any moment. "About five years ago, I was working with this other guy on homicide and one of the few cases we ran together involved this man that was killing because a voice in his head was telling him to—right down to how to get it done. About two months after the arrest, we found out the man had a tumor in his head, pushing down on something or another and messing with his brain. *That's* why he was hearing the voices and had no moral quandaries about murder. So I spent about a month talking on-again-off-again with this specialist, just to make sure we were charging this guy correctly, knowing full well that he'd walk if this medical excuse was legit.

"Anyway, it turns out it *was* legit. And I slowly started to grow sort of fascinated with how tumors can mess with people's minds. I wouldn't go so far as to say I became friends with this specialist, but I got to know him well. I've played golf with him a few times since then, nothing more than that."

Rachel looked at the card and tilted her head at Jack. It was such a simple gesture but something about it reminded her of just how good of a friend he was. She had no idea if she wouldever use the information on the card, but it was nice to know the option was there.

"And you're telling me this *why?*"

"This guy is an expert. Sort of a genius in the field of tumors. He went on and on about these experimental procedures that would be less dependent on approaches like chemo. Now...don't get mad, but I may have called him yesterday."

"Jack..."

"I told him the little bit I know about what's going on with you and he said he'd be happy to see you. All you have to do is call him."

"I appreciate it, Jack, but I don't want to spend the little bit of time I *do* have in doctor's offices."

"So don't. Call him. Go on one visit to see if he can help. It can't hurt, right?"

She took the card and tucked it away in her pocket. She wasn't sure if she'd ever use it, but she appreciated the thought. "I suppose not."

"Now, on to other things," he said. "If Peter does indeed leave you over this, would you allow me to punch him in the chin?"

"No, Jack," she knew he was going for a laugh, but she just couldn't manage one for him. "Besides, I sort of get it. I should have told him right away. But I was scared, and..."

"Hey, Rachel? Look...like I said at the hospital. This is between you and me. But I care about you and don't want to see you hurt. If it gets too far down the road and your condition gets worse—"

"I know. You'll tell Anderson if I don't."

"Damn right. So please don't put me in that position," he sighed and leaned back in his seat. He took a sip of coffee and looked earnestly at her. "Other than that, I've got your back. If you don't want it out in the public, my lips are sealed."

"I appreciate that, Jack."

"You think you'll call my guy?"

"I just don't know yet."

She watched Jack relax and sit back upright in the seat. She knew what he was about to do and was reminded of just how good of a partner he was—how good of a *friend*.

"So, I talked to Anderson this morning and he thinks there are going to be measures made pretty soon to offload some of the paperwork with reports."

"You don't have to do that."

"Do what?" he asked.

"Change the subject. It is what it is. And it sucks. But I think...I think I need to just sit in it for a while. Between now and when I have to pick up Paige, would you just sit in it with me?"

"So, like...sit and don't talk to ease the tension?"

"Yes."

He grimaced playfully and nodded, grabbing up his cup. He then made a show of narrowing his lips and keeping them tight together. Rachel smiled and looked out of the window, watching the early afternoon traffic passing by. Her mind conjured up an image of Grandma Tate on the iPad, laughing at Paige not too long after dropping a huge nugget of wisdom that was almost as loud as her father, once again rattling his old chains.

I don't want to leave any old, wilted relationships to die in a negative light...I don't want to leave anything unsaid.

And on the heels of that, she recalled the feeling that had more or less become the theme of the Brandon Holcomb case. It seemed more relevant than ever as she sat in the quiet with Jack, watching the cars roll by.

The sense that her days were numbered. The sense that she was running out of time.

CHAPTER THIRTY

Florence Tate sat on her back patio with a tall glass of sweet tea, watching the butterflies dancing over the tops of her rosebushes. Her phone was sitting on the little glass coffee table in front of her and she knew the next call she needed to make was to her son. She was starting to regret telling Rachel that she was going to reach out to him because that wasn't a burden Rachel needed to deal with. Lord knew the girl had worked hard enough to free herself from the grief of an absent father—an absent father that had been a wretched human being when he had been present.

Then again, Florence didn't really have too much time to worry about every word she spoke. Not anymore, anyway. She felt perfectly fine, but the doctors had told her that was to be expected. Apparently, when it came, it would come quick. When? No one knew, exactly but she wasn't making any long-term plans, that was for sure.

She was a bit rattled by how hard it was to pick up the stupid phone and call him, though. It hadn't been *that* long since they'd last spoken. She knew why she was hesitating, though. She knew there was a very large part of her that feared he just would not care. He'd tell her he was sorry but that would be about it. And did she really want to face that?

Her worries and thoughts were interrupted by the faint squealing of brakes. It was just after two in the afternoon and the sound of those brakes was all too familiar. It was the mailman, coming in that beat-up little white truck that needed more than just new brakes, but a paint job as well.

She got up from her chair, leaving her cellphone. Maybe the mere act of walking around the house to the mailbox would help her find the courage she needed to call her son. She walked down the patio stairs and headed around the side of the yard. Passing by the small pear tree in her side yard, she saw that the hummingbird feeder needed to be refilled. She made a note of this as she came to the front yard, just in time to see the mail truck make the very short jaunt between her house and her neighbor's.

She walked across the yard and came to her mailbox—yet another thing that could use a paintjob. She reached inside and grabbed the day's mail, walking down her sidewalk to the front door just like she

154

did every day after the mail was delivered. And, like always, she thumbed through it all on her way to the front door.

Today's mail seemed no different than the usual offerings: unsolicited mail about medical solutions and insurance, a flier for a local furniture store, the internet bill…but then something different. It was a basic, white envelope with her name handwritten in the center. There was no return address and. the weight of the envelope made it seem as if there was only a single sheet of paper inside.

Curious, she paused on her front porch and tore the envelop open. Inside was a single sheet of notebook par, folded over in thirds. Perhaps it was because she'd been thinking of her son, but when she pulled the paper out and unfolded it, she began to feel nervous.

The letter inside was not from her son. Although, as she began to slightly tremble as she read the very brief message, she rather wished it was. The letter had no formal greeting and got straight to the point. It read:

Sorry to hear you're not going to make it much longer. At least you won't go alone. Did you know RACHEL is going to be just as DEAD as you very soon?

There was no real salutation to speak of. Instead, there was an addition on the bottom right corner, scrawled as if it had been nothing more than an afterthought.

—Agent Rachel Gift's NO.1 FAN!!!

Florence read it two more times before she bothered stepping inside her house. She hurried to the back patio for her phone, though the idea of calling her son was now the farthest thing from her mind.

HER LAST FEAR
(A Rachel Gift FBI Suspense Thriller —Book 4)

Young, healthy victims are turning up dead in the New Mexico desert, their bodies displayed in dramatic ways. Rachel must race against time to track down the killer—even if that means indulging in his twisted fantasies.

FBI Special Agent Rachel Gift is among the FBI's most brilliant agents at hunting down serial killers. She plans on doing this forever—until she discovers she has months left to live. Determined to go down fighting, and to keep her diagnosis a secret, Rachel faces her own mortality while trying to save other's lives. But how long can she go until she collapses under the weight of it all?

"A MASTERPIECE OF THRILLER AND MYSTERY. Blake Pierce did a magnificent job developing characters with a psychological side so well described that we feel inside their minds, follow their fears and cheer for their success. Full of twists, this book will keep you awake until the turn of the last page."
--Books and Movie Reviews, Roberto Mattos (re Once Gone)

HER LAST FEAR (A Rachel Gift FBI Suspense Thriller) is book #4 in a long-anticipated new series by #1 bestseller and USA Today bestselling author Blake Pierce, whose bestseller Once Gone (a free download) has received over 1,000 five star reviews.

FBI Agent Rachel Gift, 33, unparalleled for her ability to enter the minds of serial killers, is a rising star in the Behavioral Crimes Unit—until a routine doctor visit reveals she has but a few months left to live.

Not wishing to burden others with her pain, Rachel decides, agonizing as it is, not to tell anyone—not even her boss, her partner, her husband, or her seven-year-old daughter. She wants to go down fighting, and to take as many serial killers with her as she can.

When she learns of a string of bizarre murders in New Mexico, Rachel quickly realizes this is no ordinary killer. In a race against time, Rachel must quickly figure out who is luring these victims out to the desert—and why.

Meanwhile, her own clock is running out. Can she solve this macabre puzzle and stop the murderer once and for all?

A riveting and chilling crime thriller featuring a brilliant and flailing FBI agent, the RACHEL GIFT series is an unputdownable mystery, packed with suspense, twists and shocking secrets, propelled by a page-turning pace that will keep you bleary-eyed late into the night.

Books #5 and #6 in the series—HER LAST CHOICE and HER LAST BREATH—are now also available!

Blake Pierce

Blake Pierce is the USA Today bestselling author of the RILEY PAGE mystery series, which includes seventeen books. Blake Pierce is also the author of the MACKENZIE WHITE mystery series, comprising fourteen books; of the AVERY BLACK mystery series, comprising six books; of the KERI LOCKE mystery series, comprising five books; of the MAKING OF RILEY PAIGE mystery series, comprising six books; of the KATE WISE mystery series, comprising seven books; of the CHLOE FINE psychological suspense mystery, comprising six books; of the JESSE HUNT psychological suspense thriller series, comprising nineteen books; of the AU PAIR psychological suspense thriller series, comprising three books; of the ZOE PRIME mystery series, comprising six books; of the ADELE SHARP mystery series, comprising thirteen books, of the EUROPEAN VOYAGE cozy mystery series, comprising four books; of the new LAURA FROST FBI suspense thriller, comprising six books (and counting); of the new ELLA DARK FBI suspense thriller, comprising nine books (and counting); of the A YEAR IN EUROPE cozy mystery series, comprising nine books, of the AVA GOLD mystery series, comprising six books (and counting); and of the RACHEL GIFT mystery series, comprising six books (and counting).

An avid reader and lifelong fan of the mystery and thriller genres, Blake loves to hear from you, so please feel free to visit www.blakepierceauthor.com to learn more and stay in touch.

BOOKS BY BLAKE PIERCE

RACHEL GIFT MYSTERY SERIES
HER LAST WISH (Book #1)
HER LAST CHANCE (Book #2)
HER LAST HOPE (Book #3)
HER LAST FEAR (Book #4)
HER LAST CHOICE (Book #5)
HER LAST BREATH (Book #6)

AVA GOLD MYSTERY SERIES
CITY OF PREY (Book #1)
CITY OF FEAR (Book #2)
CITY OF BONES (Book #3)
CITY OF GHOSTS (Book #4)
CITY OF DEATH (Book #5)
CITY OF VICE (Book #6)

A YEAR IN EUROPE
A MURDER IN PARIS (Book #1)
DEATH IN FLORENCE (Book #2)
VENGEANCE IN VIENNA (Book #3)
A FATALITY IN SPAIN (Book #4)

ELLA DARK FBI SUSPENSE THRILLER
GIRL, ALONE (Book #1)
GIRL, TAKEN (Book #2)
GIRL, HUNTED (Book #3)
GIRL, SILENCED (Book #4)
GIRL, VANISHED (Book 5)
GIRL ERASED (Book #6)
GIRL, FORSAKEN (Book #7)
GIRL, TRAPPED (Book #8)
GIRL, EXPENDABLE (Book #9)

LAURA FROST FBI SUSPENSE THRILLER
ALREADY GONE (Book #1)
ALREADY SEEN (Book #2)

ALREADY TRAPPED (Book #3)
ALREADY MISSING (Book #4)
ALREADY DEAD (Book #5)
ALREADY TAKEN (Book #6)

EUROPEAN VOYAGE COZY MYSTERY SERIES
MURDER (AND BAKLAVA) (Book #1)
DEATH (AND APPLE STRUDEL) (Book #2)
CRIME (AND LAGER) (Book #3)
MISFORTUNE (AND GOUDA) (Book #4)
CALAMITY (AND A DANISH) (Book #5)
MAYHEM (AND HERRING) (Book #6)

ADELE SHARP MYSTERY SERIES
LEFT TO DIE (Book #1)
LEFT TO RUN (Book #2)
LEFT TO HIDE (Book #3)
LEFT TO KILL (Book #4)
LEFT TO MURDER (Book #5)
LEFT TO ENVY (Book #6)
LEFT TO LAPSE (Book #7)
LEFT TO VANISH (Book #8)
LEFT TO HUNT (Book #9)
LEFT TO FEAR (Book #10)
LEFT TO PREY (Book #11)
LEFT TO LURE (Book #12)
LEFT TO CRAVE (Book #13)

THE AU PAIR SERIES
ALMOST GONE (Book#1)
ALMOST LOST (Book #2)
ALMOST DEAD (Book #3)

ZOE PRIME MYSTERY SERIES
FACE OF DEATH (Book#1)
FACE OF MURDER (Book #2)
FACE OF FEAR (Book #3)
FACE OF MADNESS (Book #4)
FACE OF FURY (Book #5)
FACE OF DARKNESS (Book #6)

A JESSIE HUNT PSYCHOLOGICAL SUSPENSE SERIES
THE PERFECT WIFE (Book #1)
THE PERFECT BLOCK (Book #2)
THE PERFECT HOUSE (Book #3)
THE PERFECT SMILE (Book #4)
THE PERFECT LIE (Book #5)
THE PERFECT LOOK (Book #6)
THE PERFECT AFFAIR (Book #7)
THE PERFECT ALIBI (Book #8)
THE PERFECT NEIGHBOR (Book #9)
THE PERFECT DISGUISE (Book #10)
THE PERFECT SECRET (Book #11)
THE PERFECT FAÇADE (Book #12)
THE PERFECT IMPRESSION (Book #13)
THE PERFECT DECEIT (Book #14)
THE PERFECT MISTRESS (Book #15)
THE PERFECT IMAGE (Book #16)
THE PERFECT VEIL (Book #17)
THE PERFECT INDISCRETION (Book #18)
THE PERFECT RUMOR (Book #19)

CHLOE FINE PSYCHOLOGICAL SUSPENSE SERIES
NEXT DOOR (Book #1)
A NEIGHBOR'S LIE (Book #2)
CUL DE SAC (Book #3)
SILENT NEIGHBOR (Book #4)
HOMECOMING (Book #5)
TINTED WINDOWS (Book #6)

KATE WISE MYSTERY SERIES
IF SHE KNEW (Book #1)
IF SHE SAW (Book #2)
IF SHE RAN (Book #3)
IF SHE HID (Book #4)
IF SHE FLED (Book #5)
IF SHE FEARED (Book #6)
IF SHE HEARD (Book #7)

THE MAKING OF RILEY PAIGE SERIES

WATCHING (Book #1)
WAITING (Book #2)
LURING (Book #3)
TAKING (Book #4)
STALKING (Book #5)
KILLING (Book #6)

RILEY PAIGE MYSTERY SERIES
ONCE GONE (Book #1)
ONCE TAKEN (Book #2)
ONCE CRAVED (Book #3)
ONCE LURED (Book #4)
ONCE HUNTED (Book #5)
ONCE PINED (Book #6)
ONCE FORSAKEN (Book #7)
ONCE COLD (Book #8)
ONCE STALKED (Book #9)
ONCE LOST (Book #10)
ONCE BURIED (Book #11)
ONCE BOUND (Book #12)
ONCE TRAPPED (Book #13)
ONCE DORMANT (Book #14)
ONCE SHUNNED (Book #15)
ONCE MISSED (Book #16)
ONCE CHOSEN (Book #17)

MACKENZIE WHITE MYSTERY SERIES
BEFORE HE KILLS (Book #1)
BEFORE HE SEES (Book #2)
BEFORE HE COVETS (Book #3)
BEFORE HE TAKES (Book #4)
BEFORE HE NEEDS (Book #5)
BEFORE HE FEELS (Book #6)
BEFORE HE SINS (Book #7)
BEFORE HE HUNTS (Book #8)
BEFORE HE PREYS (Book #9)
BEFORE HE LONGS (Book #10)
BEFORE HE LAPSES (Book #11)
BEFORE HE ENVIES (Book #12)
BEFORE HE STALKS (Book #13)

BEFORE HE HARMS (Book #14)

AVERY BLACK MYSTERY SERIES
CAUSE TO KILL (Book #1)
CAUSE TO RUN (Book #2)
CAUSE TO HIDE (Book #3)
CAUSE TO FEAR (Book #4)
CAUSE TO SAVE (Book #5)
CAUSE TO DREAD (Book #6)

KERI LOCKE MYSTERY SERIES
A TRACE OF DEATH (Book #1)
A TRACE OF MURDER (Book #2)
A TRACE OF VICE (Book #3)
A TRACE OF CRIME (Book #4)
A TRACE OF HOPE (Book #5)

Made in the USA
Las Vegas, NV
12 January 2023

65422130R00095